HELD BY A MONSTER

KENZIE KELLY

HELD BY A MONSTER
Copyright © 2024 by Kenzie Kelly.

Website & Newsletter: http://www.kenziekelly.com
Twitter: @exlibriskenzie
Instagram: @exlibiriskenzie
Facebook: kenzie kelly
Discord Readers group: the mythic menagerie

All rights reserved. No part of this publication may be reproduced, stored in a retrieval system, or transmitted in any form or by any means, electronic, mechanical, recording or otherwise, without the prior written permission of the copyright holder.

This is a work of fiction. Names, characters, businesses, places, events and incidents are either the products of the author's imagination or used in a fictitious manner. Any resemblance to actual persons, living or dead, or actual events is purely coincidental.

Cover illustration by Nyx.

Typography and formatting by Kenzie Kelly.

Chapter header illustrations by Kit Fox.

Editing by Dayna Hart.

Look, I'm not saying I'd like a seven-foot-tall werewolf/dragon hybrid to rail me in the woods, but I'm not NOT saying it either.

KENZIE KELLY

ONE

MY FOOT CAUGHT ON a root and my ankle bent to the left. I went down hard, too fast to bring my hands up and break my fall. The dirt was cool on my cheek and I thought for a minute I might just stay there. I could hear them behind me, stomping through the woods, their dogs barking. I pushed to my knees, ignored the stabs of pain in my hands, and crawled forward. I knew they would catch me, but I couldn't stop fighting.

A sob tore from my throat and I swallowed its friends.

I needed to keep moving. My ankle dragged behind me, the pain of it lost among many others.

They'd said if I reached the wire, I'd be free. I didn't really believe it, but I held on to what little hope there was. The ground gave way beneath me and I fell. I should have screamed as I rolled down a steep embankment, but my voice refused. I let the darkness take me, my eyes closing as I spun.

Branches tore at my hair and the thin shirt they'd given me. I gathered new scrapes and bruises from rocks and roots. I came to a sudden stop when my stomach hit a tree, my body folding around it. The trunk was warm and soft...

And it moved.

I struggled to open my eyes. I wanted to see what I rested against, but my eyelids were so heavy. I'd stopped running and without the momentum I'd stalled. My muscles no longer wanted to work.

Warm, strong arms slipped under me and lifted. My head lolled, my neck refusing to work. The arm shifted under my shoulders and cradled my head. I couldn't work out what took over for my neck. Too big to be a hand, too wide to be an elbow.

The dogs barked and I whimpered.

A growl unlike any I'd ever heard bloomed at my side.

I should be afraid.

The thought wandered through my brain like a wraith. Fleeting and without substance. It wasn't fear the vibration made me feel—it was safety. Somehow, I knew the growl wasn't meant for me.

I felt air rushing over the bare skin of my legs and arms. I didn't care where the thing took me, as long as it was away from the dogs. Away from the men that stalked me through the trees. Away from the evil that waited for me when I was caught.

The air changed and grew colder. The sweat on my heated skin cooled and I shivered. The arms tightened around me. I still didn't know where we were. My eyes refused to open. From the sound, we were in an enclosed space. Maybe a house?

Outside it was sweltering. Even in the middle of the night, it was hot.

I wished I could shut my brain off. Give myself to the darkness and pass out. I didn't care what happened to me now. It couldn't be worse than what they'd done to me.

We dropped suddenly, my stomach flying into my throat. I squeaked and managed to get an eye open. Dark. Nothing but unrelenting black.

After we landed with barely a jolt, a voice said, "Shh, little one. You're safe now."

A voice so deep I felt it in my bones. Male, but I didn't cringe. I believed him.

He carried me for what seemed like miles, twisting and turning. I'd open my eyes every so often, but unable to see even the smallest detail I gave up.

I heard the trickle of water, and swallowed. My throat was so dry it hurt. I wanted to ask him to stop, to let me drink, but I couldn't form the words. I peeled my tongue from the roof of my mouth and opened my lips with a sigh.

"That water isn't good. Just a little further."

Was he reading my mind? Did I care?

I heard the air shift again, soft sounds echoing around a large chamber. I cracked an eye open and blinked against the light. My vision cleared and I stared in shock. Five creatures…beasts…monsters…stared back. They were arranged around a thick, raw edged table covered in papers and open laptops.

They were massive. Easily standing seven feet tall with heads like wolves. Their ears pointed and the crown of their heads sprouted curling horns that swept up and back. Long arms ended in gigantic hands, the fingers tipped with two-inch claws. Wide chests narrowed to waists that split into muscled thighs. They stood on paws with claws longer than the ones on their fingers.

They were covered in fur everywhere except their bellies. The smooth skin there showed off muscles so defined they put bodybuilders to shame. Their eyes seemed to glow gold, red, or blue. Their fur ranged in color from darkest black to light gray and most had their heads tilted. Strange white markings were on each of their right wrists.

As one, their snouts lifted to look at the one carrying me. The one centered on the far side of the table broke the silence.

"Drym?"

Seeing them was confusing. They resembled wild beasts more than anything human, and what little adrenaline I had left should have pumped through my veins, urging me to run. Instead, I felt calmer and safer cradled in the arms of this creature than I had in a long time.

"I found her. She's…mine?"

"Right, I can see that. I'm not asking you to give her up, just on how you came by her. Will she be missed?"

The one carrying me shifted from one foot to the other. "I don't know."

The other sighed and pinched his snout between his eyes. It was such a human thing to do, to pinch the nose in thought.

"Does she speak?"

"She is able, but I believe she has been running for some time. She needs water, food and rest."

One of the others moved then, one with blue eyes, and stalked toward me with the grace of a cat. The arms around me squeezed and they moved back a step. I grunted as the air was crushed out of my lungs and immediately they released.

The blue-eyed one stopped several feet away. "She is injured, Drym. I only seek to render aid."

"Don't touch."

The snarl stunned me. These were obviously his friends or family. Why was he so protective of me? Was I like a treat he didn't want to share? Was he going to eat me?

My heartbeat sped, thumping against my chest. The crack and crunch of bones sounded in my mind and my panic spiraled out of control.

Finally, the darkness closed in and sucked me under.

TWO

"YOU SCARED HER, CAVI!" I snarled and snapped my teeth at my brother. If this female weren't in my arms, I would sink my teeth in his belly.

"Drym!"

Kragen's sharp voice turned my head to him.

"We are not the enemy. We will not hurt your female. It's clear she needs care. Let us help you."

My arms pulsed. They were right, of course. I needed to let them help, but some instinct wanted to keep them away. I shook my head, my tail thrashing behind me. My words came out as a whine. "I know she needs help. I just can't. I can't put her down."

I dropped my head in shame. This female needed help and I was keeping her from it.

We had always worked together, the six of us. We were made at the same time and grew at the same rate. We learned quickly that each of us had a skill that complemented the others. As a team, we were unstoppable.

Kragen nodded in understanding. "Okay, we'll work with that, but Cavi needs to get close to look her over."

I growled louder; the sound bouncing off the walls of the cave.

Kragen's patience snapped. "Her blood coats the air, Drym!"

My growl stuttered into a whine.

Kragen's eyes flicked over my shoulder and he dipped his muzzle. I felt the sting of a needle and sighed in relief. A sedative wouldn't affect me long—no medicine did—but it would calm me enough to let Cavi see to her.

Cavi was in front of me in a blink and gently took her from my arms. My limbs were heavy but I tracked his tiniest movement. He laid her on the table, scanned her quickly, and then barked orders.

"Quin, grab a suture kit. Some of these cuts are deep. Thurl, start cleaning her feet."

Kragen stayed next to me. Lending me support, but also there in case I needed to be restrained. Cavi started at her head and cleaned her wounds as he came to them.

"Scratches, mostly."

"She was running through the woods, panicked," I told them what little I knew. "There were men and dogs after her."

A collective growl filled the air as we all reacted to her being hunted. None of us liked to see harm come to a female.

They had put females in with us, of course, even before we reached maturity. They wanted to see if we would breed them or kill them. We refused to do either.

Roul went a little mad from the tests. The females he was given were always terrified, no matter what he did to calm them.

He was the largest of us, and his red eyes revealed his purpose. Aggression. Force. He and Thurl were true weapons. The tip of the sword. Kragen and I were the wielders. Bred for intelligence and strategy, we planned. We saw all avenues and possibilities before we landed on the best way to accomplish a mission.

Cavi and Quin were our healers. Cavi was better in emergencies, field triage. Quin kept us healthy and saw to any long-term care that was needed.

That wasn't to say we weren't all deadly. We were. They tested us for that, too. Forced us to fight for our lives, or that of our brothers.

Quin had cleaned her left arm and given her a local anesthetic so he could sew a deep gash in her bicep.

I wanted to rip his head off.

"I don't understand, Kragen. Why do I feel like this? This never happened with the other females." I wrapped my hand over my eyes to block the sight of her in pain, but not looking was worse.

"I don't know, Drym. When she's stable, we'll have Quin draw blood. Maybe it will provide answers."

"We should have left one of the scientists alive." Red edged my vision and I took a deep breath. I couldn't lose control. Not while she was near.

Roul had moved to my other side, just in case. "We did," he snapped.

Yes, but none of us knew what happened to her after we escaped. It caused Roul pain to even mention her. I wouldn't have normally been so careless. "Why do you think they were hunting her?"

Kragen shook his head. "I don't know."

HELD BY A MONSTER

"Roul," I flicked an ear at him but couldn't look away from the female. "Can you track them? Find out what they were doing?"

He spun and I heard his claws scrape the rock beneath our feet as he took off.

Kragen called after him, "Do not engage!"

All we received in response was a grunt.

Cavi had finished cleaning her face, neck, upper chest, and right arm. He moved to the torn hem of the shirt she wore and lifted it. I took a step forward. Kragen threw his arm in front of me.

"I think we should let Drym check her torso in private. He can clean her, and if there are any wounds that need care beyond what he can provide, he will let us know." Kragen grabbed my snout. "Right?"

"Yes. Yes, that would be better." Tension eased from me as Cavi dropped her shirt and began to clean her legs. I didn't like them touching her at all, but my control was getting better.

Her eyes flew open and her head whipped around. She thrashed and the others held her limbs. My vision was well into the red and I ripped through Kragen's hold and moved to her, batting Quin aside.

Her eyes hit mine and I crouched next to her. "Shh, little one. You are safe."

"Are you real?"

I didn't want her to fear me. I didn't want her to scream and throw herself into the corner and make herself as small as possible.

But I couldn't lie to her. "Yes, we are real."

Her chest rose as she inhaled, her eyes closing on an exhale. "Thank god."

We all looked at each other in shock. That was not a reaction we'd ever gotten before. She relaxed, so Quin and Thurl released her and resumed cleaning her legs.

"Can you tell us what happened?" Kragen slipped a bottle of water into my hand.

I twisted the cap and offered it to her. She struggled to sit up, so I put my hand between her shoulder blades and supported her. I wanted to shout for joy when she leaned into my touch. She drained the entire bottle.

"Thank you." She took a deep breath. "I was kidnapped after work, taken to a house and kept in a basement with other women. The men hunted us."

"Why?" I couldn't keep the anger from my voice. I saw it reflected in her eyes.

"Sport. Boredom. Because they could. Who knows why twisted rich men do anything?"

She looked at each of us before her eyes landed back on me. "You guys really are enormous, hunh?"

I chuckled. "Yes. I am Drym."

"Hi, Drym. I'm Kendal."

I went around the same way she had studied each of us. "This is Kragen, Cavi, Thurl and Quin. Our brother Roul is investigating the men who chased you."

"Good." Her features hardened. "I hope he kills every one of them."

KENZIE KELLY

THREE

THESE BEASTS LOOKED LIKE they could kill the entire house full of men without breaking a sweat. I meant what I said. I wanted them dead.

Fury whipped through me, heating my skin and tensing my muscles.

"Try to relax." A lighter gray with blue eyes, this one was Cavi. I blew out through pursed lips and attempted to do as he asked. It was easier when I looked at Drym. His gold eyes calmed me. Maybe because he'd saved me, or maybe because he looked at me like I was precious.

He had carried me in his arms, his hands so gentle.

I barely felt a whisper when he used one of his wicked-looking claws to hook a lock of hair that had fallen in my face and push it back. He smoothed the back of his finger down my cheek, and that small kindness turned my anger to relief.

"You smell sad. Why?"

Tears leaked from my eyes and I reached my hand to the side of his face and buried my fingers in his fur. He was warm and soft and the tears came harder. "Because I feel safe, and my mind is dealing with all the fear I've held at bay."

He nodded. "Yes, you are safe."

He tilted his head, and I buried my fingers further into his ruff.

"Would you like more water? Are you hungry?"

"Water would be nice." They didn't withhold water or food, but I'd been running a long time before I ran into Drym.

Another bottle appeared in front of me, the cap already off. I sipped this one slower. "I don't mean to be rude, but what are you guys? I mean, without the horns and tail, I'd say you were werewolves, but I didn't think anything like that existed. Guess you're living proof I was wrong."

"They called us wyrfangs, but you're right, we aren't wolves, or werewolves, or dragons. We are all of them."

I looked around at each of them again. "I don't follow. Who is 'they'? What do you mean you aren't them, but you are? And hold up—dragons? Really?"

HELD BY A MONSTER

The other golden-eyed beast sighed and nodded at Drym. "We knew we'd have to explain to someone, sometime. This moves our timeline up, but perhaps she can help us with what our next step should be."

"Yes, those creatures exist, and we suspect, many more."

"Holy crap. Dragons." Mind blown, I shook my head to get back on track. "Who is this 'they'?"

"*They* were scientists. They created us, raised us, trained us." Drym looked at the others. "Tortured us." He held up his right hand and turned the inside of his wrist toward me. "Branded us."

The marks on their wrists were a brand? They'd been marked like cattle? A sinking feeling that their story was much worse than I could imagine hit my gut, but I didn't interrupt.

"From the moment we were born to surrogates, they taught us to hunt and evade. They taught us to survive. They tested our limits. We are a blend of creatures, a mix of DNA spliced into a single embryo. Whatever they thought would make the best weapons, they used. Dragon and werewolf, mainly, but we honestly don't know beyond that."

"No one stopped them? I thought the government oversaw all labs doing genetic modification. Actually, I thought those kinds of experiments were illegal."

Drym's head tilted toward me, his ears pricked forward. "Is hunting human women legal?"

I laughed, the sound so rusty it startled me. "You have an excellent point."

A massive wyrfang entered the cave, and although I felt comfortable around the others, this one was different. More menacing, deadlier. His red eyes glowed, and when they lit on me, they narrowed in anger. I shrank and Drym moved to block me from him.

"Report." That was Kragen. He had an air of confidence and control about him that branded him as the leader.

His growl was so deep, I could barely understand him. "Tracked them to a house. It looks nice until you look into the basement. One tiny window with bars. It's a gods damned prison in there."

I nodded. "Yeah, that's where they kept us."

"Us? There are more females there?" Drym's ears were flat against his head.

I blinked to stem more tears. "There were. I was the only one left."

I was suddenly smooshed against Drym's soft chest, his skin like velvet over steel. His fur was shorter here, showing off the sculpted muscles in his chest. I sank into him.

I should have been screaming and running as fast as my legs would carry me, but I felt ... safe. For the first time in a long while. They were weapons, Drym had said as much. They certainly looked like they could rip me in half without breaking a sweat. But I wasn't afraid of them.

"And the men?"

Roul's eyes seemed to flare darker, brighter, a blood-red glow that made him seem even more dangerous than before. "The house was empty."

"Fucking cowards ran." I was angry they weren't all dead.

Quin stepped around so he was facing me. "Is there anyone we can call?"

"No. We figured out none of us had families that would file missing persons reports. They were careful, calculated."

"Oh, thank fuck."

The two closest to him slugged him none too gently in each arm.

"Ow! What was that for? You know as well as I do we would have had to tie Drym up if she wanted to leave. Either that, or figure out real quick how we were going to break our existence to the entire human populous."

The gigantic newcomer grumbled at him. "Shut up, you idiot."

"What? At least I asked. None of you other imbeciles thought to see if she had people worried sick about her."

"Yeah, but you didn't have to sound so happy she didn't." Cavi said as he packed away his first aid kit.

Kragen's voice cut above the rest. "Drym, maybe you should take her to a room and let her rest?"

I couldn't tell if the rumble beneath my ear was humor or irritation.

"That's probably best."

He scooped me into his arms with ease, so careful not to rub any of my scrapes or the bandage covering the cut they'd sutured. The kindness and care I was getting from these beasts—these wyrfangs—was more than I'd had in months.

I swiped at his chest, smearing my tears over his skin. He leaned over me and I felt his muzzle against my back. His body almost completely enveloped me and I'd never felt more cherished or protected.

FOUR

WE FOUND THIS CAVE by happenstance. And when I say happenstance, I mean Quin was walking backwards while running his mouth and dropped into a hole when the ground gave way beneath him.

It was an extensive cave system, with the large chamber that fit all of us comfortably, and smaller offshoots where we could have our own space.

We'd never had our own space before. There's no privacy when the walls are glass, and the eyes of cameras always track you.

At first, it was too quiet. We were used to the sounds of scientists coming and going, lab machinery whirring, each other's movements and other small noises. After a week, we grew more comfortable with ourselves and could spend more time apart.

I set her on the nest of blankets I'd made in the corner and turned a lamp on low for her to see. It wasn't much, but I'd salvaged several thick foam sheets that cushioned it from the rock floor. The blankets were soft and warm.

"I would have spruced up if I'd known I'd have company." I kept my tone light, sensing she needed to get the darkness out of her mind. I couldn't imagine what she'd been through.

She smiled, and I grinned.

Then she laughed. A beautiful sound I wanted to hear again and again. Wait, was she laughing at me? My head tilted and my ears drooped.

"I'm sorry, it's just…" She shook her head. "I know you're smiling, but to me, it looks like you're showing a lot of teeth. It should scare the crap out of me, but I find it adorable."

She found me… endearing? My grin grew and she laughed again, but I didn't mind. I would grin as wide as I could to hear that sound.

"Why aren't you? Scared of us, I mean. We tried so hard to not frighten the women, but they all screamed and cried."

"Drym, are you saying they put women in with you? Why?"

I crouched until I could sit on the floor. I shrugged. "To see what we would do."

She sucked in a breath and reached for me. I stretched out my arm and stared as she wrapped her fingers around my hand. My entire body lit up like I was in the fog only, I wasn't angry. I felt something, but I wasn't sure what it was. The only other time I'd felt this happy was when we knew we'd escaped, when we knew we'd destroyed them.

"What did you do?"

I snorted. "We tried to look as small as possible. As harmless as possible. You can imagine how that worked out."

"I am so sorry. That sounds horrible."

I was stunned. She just escaped a terrifying situation and she was comforting me? I snuffled. "Not as awful as being hunted in the woods, I imagine."

She shook her head. "That was awful, but they took me two weeks ago. You lived your entire life in captivity. I can't imagine the trauma you've experienced."

I'd never thought of it that way. Trauma. It was just how it was. It was all we'd ever known. We knew we wanted out, wanted freedom, wanted control over our lives and bodies.

She cleared her throat. "How did you—I mean if it's not too invasive to ask—how did you escape?"

"We'd still be there if not for one of the scientists. She was new, and I suspect she had no idea what she'd signed up for. The first time they brought her to our wing, she almost fainted.

They made fun of her, and we all got mad." I chuckled. "She found her backbone soon enough. She didn't like what they were doing, but they said it was no different from any other lab animal, and that their experiments were for the betterment of all humanity.

"Isabelle believed them, at first. Then she realized we weren't brainless beasts. That we were sentient. She started making plans, passing notes to Roul since she worked with him the most. Over the course of a month, one scribbled note at a time, we formulated a plan."

She nodded. "She helped you escape."

"Yes. We owe her everything."

"Where is she?"

I hung my head. "We don't know. The escape got … messy." Visions of men and women in white coats screaming as we tore them apart, blood coating the walls, the floor, the ceiling—us. Our claws swept through equipment, computers, storage vials. We left nothing behind. Nothing that could recreate the 'experiment' that made us. "We lost her in the confusion. She disappeared. I think she went into hiding, same as us, and is just trying to figure out what to do next."

"Roul—he must be the scary one."

I laughed. "Yes, that describes him perfectly. He likes nothing more than to rip heads, but he's fiercely loyal and protective to a fault." I sighed. "He reacted to her, like I react to you."

She laid down and snuggled into the blankets and my heart raced at seeing her comfortable in my bed. She yawned so wide I heard her jaw crack.

She hummed. "I'm sorry. I'm exhausted."

"I will leave you to sleep."

She sat straight up, panic on her face. "No! Please, don't leave. I don't want to be alone."

"Then I will stay."

She scooted to the front of the bed and patted the space she'd made behind her. I laid down, careful of my claws, horns, and the spikes on my tail. She half rolled toward me and grabbed my forearm, dragging it over her stomach. I pulled her closer and curled myself around her, silently letting her know I'd protect her from any threat.

She was asleep in moments.

With her scent in my nose, it took me a lot longer.

FIVE

I WOKE IN INCREMENTS. I knew I was in a cave with a beast at my back, but it felt so good. I couldn't remember a time I had felt so warm and safe. I hadn't been able to sleep in the cage, not really. We would take turns watching over each other, but none of us slept well or long.

Drym's chest rose and fell against my back, the rhythm steady. His arm caged me next to him, but it felt nice knowing anyone who came for me would need to go through him.

There was a hard length pressed against my ass. Surely it wasn't what I thought it was? I hadn't seen genitalia of any kind on any of them yesterday, and they hadn't been wearing clothes. It sure felt like a cock, though. A very long, very hard one.

Desire shocked me to stillness. I was getting aroused thinking about a monster's cock. I giggled.

What if it wasn't, though? What if it was just, I didn't know, a leg bone or something?

I slowly rolled under his arm, trying not to wake him up but wanting—needing—to get a look at what was poking at me. When it finally came into view, I gasped.

Definitely a monster's monster cock. It curled up toward his navel and was longer than any penis I'd ever seen—even in porn. I noticed the sides of a slit cradling the base. That must be why I didn't see anything before. They must be hidden inside when they weren't hard. It was thick at the base and tapered to a slight spade-shaped head, with short spikes running in a spiral along the entire length.

Were they hard or soft? What would *that* feel like inside me? Would it even fit inside me? Oh my god, what was I thinking?

My eyes flew up and I was pinned in place by his stare. My cheeks flamed. He'd caught me staring at his dick. What the fuck was wrong with me? I had to break the awkward silence, but I didn't think, "hey, can I touch your cock?" would be a good opener.

I swallowed. "Good morning."

He growled and moved. One minute, he was lying on his side behind me and the next, his entire snout was pressed against my pussy and he was inhaling great lungfuls of air.

I squeaked and pushed at his horns. "Hey! Hey! What are you doing?"

"Smells good. Delicious."

I quit my hands' useless attempts to push him off and covered my face.

He snuffled in closer. He practically had his nose inside me at this point. I'm sure he would have if I wasn't wearing underwear.

"Your pussy is delectable. I want to lick it."

His eyes were glowing when they looked up at me. My breath caught and my mouth went dry.

"Can I lick it?"

Oh, what the hell. How many times in a girl's life did a beast ask to lick her pussy? I would have laughed but as soon as I nodded he yanked my underwear down my legs and stroked his tongue through my slit. When it hit my clit I nearly levitated.

"Mmm, so good."

Warm flickers of his tongue popped my eyes open to see what was happening and, by all things holy, his tongue was *forked*.

He ate my cunt like a starving man who'd wandered the desert for months. His tongue dipped in and out, flicked inside me like nothing I'd ever felt and then licked in long strokes from stem to stern. Every time he hit my clit I gasped and twitched. It didn't take him long to figure out how to make me scream.

My walls clamped onto his tongue and he growled, pushing my orgasm almost to the point of pain. Oh, but it hurt so good.

Spent and panting, I threw my forearm over my eyes and groaned. Maybe I was disassociating because I'd just been through a very traumatic experience. Maybe I was in a coma and hallucinating the seven-foot-tall werewolf with horns and a forked tongue.

Whatever was happening, I knew one thing: I wanted to fuck this monster.

I pulled on his horns until he slid up to lie next to me. He licked his lips.

"None of the others smelled like you. None of the others made me want to taste. Why do you smell so good? Why do you taste like honeysuckle?"

"Um... probably because I'm turned on and you just gave me an incredible orgasm?"

His snout tipped down and he inhaled. "I want to do it again."

I grabbed his ear before he could move. "Hang on, big guy. I get to play too."

His head cocked in the most adorable way, betraying the canine portion of his DNA. I scooted until my hand brushed against his cock and he jerked. "Shh, it's okay."

HELD BY A MONSTER

He watched what I did with glowing eyes. I ran my fingers over his length, the skin warm and soft over a rigid core. The spikes were flexible, but not floppy. They felt like cartilage. My already drenched pussy flooded.

It wasn't easy to get a good grip on him with the spikes, but I figured out how to wrap my fingers between them and squeezed. I couldn't tell if his sharp intake of breath was pleasure or pain so I looked into his eyes and found them hooded. "Yes?" I asked.

"Yes," he groaned.

I twisted and slid my hand to his base before reversing course to the head. It was slick with pre-cum. I gathered it in my palm and let it ease my hand's movement. The third time I hit the base, I felt something new. The area around the upper edges of his slit opening was bigger. I got closer to get a better look at the now pronounced bump. I ran my fingers lightly around it and Drym gasped.

"What is this?"

"My opening. Our cocks stay hidden, like a dragon's."

"I gathered as much. I mean, why is this part getting bigger?" I was fascinated.

"That is my vestigial knot."

I stilled. "Your what now?"

He chuckled. "My vestigial knot. The scientists talked a good deal about our anatomy. The wolves they used for our DNA knot their partners, locking them together. We don't have a true knot, but we develop this bump at the top of our slits."

After a bit of mental calculation, I swallowed. That bump would be about clit level if they were to have penetrative sex. "How long does it stay?"

"I'm not sure. I've never come inside a partner."

SIX

HER DELICIOUS SMELL INTENSIFIED and I knew more liquid coated her cunt. Her body was easing the way for me, and it took locking every muscle to keep from plowing into her.

I couldn't keep from touching her, but when I tried again to lower my snout, she held me still. I did the next best thing and wrapped my tail around her thigh, prodding at her bundle of nerves with the sensitive tip.

She jerked forward with a gasp and whipped her head around, trying to see what I was doing with wide eyes. "What is that?"

"My tail. Since you won't let me lap at the honeysuckle making my mouth water, I will coat my tail in it."

I slid the soft underside scales along the length of her; the warmth combining with her hand on my cock forcing my eyes closed in ecstasy. Her hand jerked tight when I pushed inside her, flicking against her inner walls.

She whimpered, her other hand grabbing my shoulder as she turned onto her side toward me.

The new position closed her legs, and that wouldn't do. I grabbed the back of her knee and drew her leg up and over mine, spreading her wide and giving me plenty of access. Her scent flooded the cave and I slurped at the drool flooding my mouth.

I pushed my tail deeper and her hand spasmed as if she'd lost control of her movements. I should stop. She'd been traumatized, caged for weeks. I pushed my nose next to her ear, inhaling her scent.

"Tell me to stop now, or I am going to fuck you." I held still, waiting for her to stop me.

She wiggled in my arms, her voice low when she finally said, "Don't stop."

I raised her chin with a finger and stared into her desire clouded eyes. "You are sure?"

She swallowed and nodded.

I grabbed her wrists and drew them over her head, securing them with one hand as I rolled her onto her back and settled between her thighs. My cock notched effortlessly at her entrance and I pushed forward, going as slow as I was able. I felt every single one of my short spikes enter her and it was all I could do not to split her open with one thrust.

It was a slow, painful slide into her tight sheath. I groaned when my slit hit her. I bit out between gritted teeth, "You are so tight. So perfect."

"I can't believe you fit. I feel like one wrong move and you'll shred me from the inside."

I pulled out halfway and pushed back in. Both of us groaned. "There are no wrong moves."

I took up the task of rubbing her clit with my knot while running my tongue up the side of her neck. More of her honey flooded over me and the slide in and out of her was easier then. I picked up the pace. "I'm going to fill you with my cum."

She moaned and I curved my spine to put space between us. I released her hands and lifted her head.

"Look at how good you take me. You were made for me."

Tremors gripped my cock and she screamed. Her orgasm urged me on, and it wasn't long before I followed. I buried myself deep within her and felt my knot swell even more, pressing against her and giving her another wave of ecstasy.

I wished I had lasted longer. I wanted to do so much more with her. Learn every inch of her body. Mark her as mine.

There was plenty of time for that later. I never intended to let her go.

As her breathing slowed and her hands dug into the fur on my arms I growled, "Mine."

"I belong to no one."

Her voice was full of venom and my ears flattened against my head. I felt her pull away. I searched her face for any clue to what I'd done to upset her. I couldn't help the whine that whistled through my nose.

"Don't." She turned her face away.

"What do I do?" My chest felt like it was caving in. "How do I make you soft and warm again?"

She chuckled but it held no humor. "You can't. You fucked up thinking you could claim me like some porcelain doll—some possession. I am not something to be owned!"

My entire body shrank. "I didn't mean it like that."

"Oh?" She spat her words at me. "How did you mean it?"

"I meant you were mine because I am yours. You hold my heart, body, and soul in your hands to do with what you wish. I am yours to command. Yours to touch. Yours to use. Yours to wound."

I wanted to wipe myself from her thighs, clean her and hold her, but she pushed away from me. I sat back on my haunches and curled into myself.

Ask me to kill someone and I did it without hesitation. Not knowing what to do or how to act was foreign and uncomfortable. She stared at me for a long while and I thought she might invite me back into her arms. I swayed toward her and she winced.

"I just…" She ran a hand over her face and huffed. "Can you leave? I can't look at you right now."

Pain seared through me. Her voice was small, defeated. In the short time I'd known her, she'd never given up. I had done this. I had taken her where two weeks in confinement and being hunted hadn't. I strangled the whine that threatened in my throat and stood.

I hesitated before disappearing down the tunnel. "I won't go far… if you need anything…" My throat closed as I walked back to my brothers, giving her the space she'd asked for.

KENZIE KELLY

SEVEN

IT WAS TOO MUCH, too fast and it all caught up to me. The reality of everything that happened crashed over me like a tsunami when I'd heard him growl that I was his. I couldn't shake the idea that he meant to possess me, like some sort of prize. Or a hunter's trophy.

It wasn't fair to him, and I knew it, but I wasn't capable of sorting through my emotions at that moment.

The fear when I'd been kidnapped, the panic when I was thrown into the basement and the other women explained what the men had planned for me. The determination to survive, losing hope at that happening as, one by one, they took the women out and they never returned.

Sarah, Grace, Catherine. I would remember their names.

Evading the hunters long enough to think I might make it to the wire, and knowing it didn't matter if I did. Falling and being rescued by a beast. A monster I should have been more terrified of than the hunters, but I only felt safe.

Tears poured down my face and I gave in to everything at once.

It took most of an hour for me to calm down enough to think clearly about my situation. The men had gone to a lot of trouble to kidnap me. They had spent a fortune setting up the house and grounds for their sick entertainment. With that kind of sunk cost fallacy in full effect, I had to believe they would want me back.

I'd be safest staying there, with the monsters who sheltered me. With Drym.

But I couldn't turn a blind eye to what those men were doing—what it was clear they'd been doing for a long time. The evidence we hadn't been the first was in the cells where we were kept. Broken bits of painted fingernails, crude hash marks keeping time. I needed to alert the authorities. They would do it again, to another woman.

The thought turned my stomach.

I had to go home. The idea terrified me, but the decision strengthened my will. Those men would not get away with what they'd done. I would make sure of that.

HELD BY A MONSTER

A twinge of sadness hit as I thought of leaving the beasts behind. Kragen had said something about me being able to help them. I would do what I could to repay their kindness.

I was going to need so much therapy after this.

I stood and walked to the edge of the light. "Drym?" My voice was ragged from crying so I cleared my throat to try again. Before I could, he stepped out of the darkness. I backed up a step. He towered over me and I craned my neck to look up at him.

"What do you need, little one?"

He looked so eager, like a puppy who'd just heard his first 'good boy.' I almost started crying again when I remembered the look on his face when I'd gotten angry.

I rubbed at my chest. "I wanted to apologize. It was wrong of me to lash out at you."

He was shaking his head before I finished.

"I am at fault. I never should have pushed you. You have been through so much... I deserve your anger."

"No, you don't." I sighed. "But I'm too tired to argue over who's at fault. I need to go home."

He startled, and then I watched him deflate. It's hard to explain, but it was like some of the life drained out of him.

"Of course."

He looked away and I had to swallow hard not to take it back. To say I'd stay. It had to be the trauma, making me feel this way. Didn't it? I cleared my throat again. "Kragen said something about me being able to help you? I'd like to try, before I go."

The tips of his forked tongue flicked from between his teeth a few times and I thought I heard his teeth clack together.

"We would be grateful for the help."

I had no idea what help I could offer them, but I'd do what I could.

It didn't take long after rejoining the others to understand what they needed. They had been kept like lab rats for their entire lives. They only had vague intel that the director of the lab remained at large, and that an entire second society existed, one made of supernatural creatures—including the werewolves and dragons they'd been created from.

My head spun by the time Kragen went over what they knew, and what they needed.

Isabelle—the witch who'd facilitated their escape—seemed disturbed by what was happening. They had to hope that this secret society of supernaturals didn't know of their existence, or the experiments that led to it. That they would shelter them, if only they could make contact.

When he finished telling me everything they knew, I sadly shook my head. "I'm afraid I won't be able to help find them.

Until you, I had no idea supernaturals existed outside books and movies." I watched all of their muzzles drop toward the papers scattered on the table. "I bet, if I put out feelers, someone will find me. It can't be accidental that average humans don't know about creatures living among us. There have to be people who work to make sure word doesn't spread."

Drym was shaking his head. "If that's the case, talking about us to draw them out would put you in danger."

I caught his eyes and held them. "It's the least I can do after you saved my life."

He stood across the table from me, but I could hear the low growl rumble through him. Quin punched him in the arm, and the noise cut off.

"We can watch from the shadows. That way, you'll be safe, and if someone reveals themselves, we'll be there to ask for help."

The others nodded in agreement.

It was no surprise when Drym spoke. "I'll go."

Kragen was shaking his head. "It's hard enough to hide looking like we do. It'll have to be Cavi or Quin. Their eyes are easiest to hide."

Drym snarled, but in the end, relented. Before I knew it, Quin was leading me to the surface. As I passed Drym, he brushed my arm with the back of his hand.

"Be safe."

I couldn't speak past the lump in my throat, so I nodded. It had to be the trauma making me feel like my heart was being ripped from my chest as I walked further away.

Right?

EIGHT

KRAGEN RELENTED THE DAY after she left and let me follow them. I was miserable and listening to me whine was making my brothers miserable. I was instructed to be smart, and the moment I thought I could no longer be smart, I was to get back to the cave.

I'd have agreed to gnawing my arm off if it meant I could see her again.

Just the sight of her calmed me. I spent three nights staring at her window. She lived on the fourth floor of an apartment building. Quin told me which one was hers. Then he pointed to an oak tree that would conceal me and give me an almost perfect view of her.

He said he didn't tell her I was there, but each night before she turned off her lights, she stood at that window and looked out.

I knew why I couldn't go to her. We couldn't risk being exposed. Not until we knew whether the other supernaturals would accept us. The company behind our creation knew we were free. We knew they would try to capture us again. We were too valuable to them. The director would be furious we had escaped before they could truly field test our abilities.

They'd scheduled our first international mission. The scientists had brought in military commanders to watch us during an exercise. We could hear them talking about us with so much violent delight it turned our stomachs. One of them was so turned on, we could smell his arousal.

They said they were going to send us where no one would care about the people who died. We were to kill innocents, just to prove how effective we were. We knew we were weapons, that much was clear even before we'd learned what we were. Even though our treatment wasn't soft or caring, we always thought we'd be working for the good guys. We appeased our conscience telling ourselves we'd be killing bad people. Ridding the world of evil.

We'd plotted our escape for years, but that day it became clear we needed to gain our freedom before we were sent on that mission.

Fog clouded my peripheral vision and I shook my head.

I took a deep breath and slowly let it out. I focused on Kendal's window, remembering the feel of her soft curves beneath my hands and her warm cunt gripping my cock.

The fog receded.

The wind shifted, and an unfamiliar scent caught my attention. I scanned the area upwind until I caught movement. Something separated from the shadows and crept toward the building. Something that moved with supernatural speed and grace.

Each night, a different creature came. Kendal had called the police as soon as she was home. Quin was close enough to hear their conversation, and though she kept the part of monsters rescuing her to herself, she let enough hints drop about unexplained happenings to get the attention of any supernatural monitoring.

The next day, she called a therapist and let even more details drop. She said she suspected her kidnappers had drugged her, giving her hallucinations to explain seeing werewolves and dragons. Clearly it worked.

Quin was inside, in a small maintenance alcove on the same floor as Kendal. I knew whatever crept toward her, wouldn't make it by him.

I dropped out of the tree anyway, my movements faster, quieter, and more precise than its had been. I stayed downwind and far enough behind, it never saw me. The others had turned and left after standing in the lobby for a few minutes.

This one went directly to her floor. I waited as it paused in front of Kendal's door, nodding to Quin as he stepped into view.

The creature was small, and even though it had speed and its movements were fluid, it seemed little threat. No claws, no apparent fangs. If it weren't for the smell, it would seem human. A rather oddly shaped human, with long arms and short legs, but human enough to not garner undue attention. It stepped up to her door and rapped twice with its fist.

I leaned forward, balancing my weight, ready to spring if need be.

The door opened and then stopped, held to a small crack by a length of chain. My nostrils filled with Kendal's scent and my focus narrowed.

"Yes?"

Her voice was clear, strong. She sounded better than she had before, and she looked healthier from what little I could see.

"I understand you have questions about things you might have seen. There are proper channels for having such questions answered. Protocols that must be followed. You understand?"

She nodded and the creature offered her a white envelope.

"I am here to extend an invitation to meet with a representative."

"You can leave it on the ground, please."

Pride swelled my chest. My female was smart.

The creature did as she asked and gave a curt bow before leaving the way it had come. Quin and I stepped back into the shadows and watched until it was clear of the building. Kendal's door closed and I heard the rattle of the chain before it opened wide. She stepped into the opening and grinned.

"Come in, you two. You'll ruin it if the neighbors see you."

NINE

I KNEW QUIN WAS there. I'd offered to let him stay in the apartment with me, but he'd refused with such vehemence that it tipped me to the fact Drym must be nearby as well. It didn't take me long to work out where he was hiding.

Just knowing he was there made me feel better, which was absurd. My therapist confirmed that my attachment to my "mystery" rescuer was a trauma response. I tried to see it that way, but it didn't feel right.

I can't imagine a trauma response caused people to have incredibly dirty, sexy dreams every time their eyes closed. They were getting ridiculous. I'd even asked Quin if they had any psychic powers, thinking maybe Drym was in my head somehow. His ears had flopped to the side when he said no and it was so damn adorable I'd wanted to ruffle the fur on his head.

My entire world had shifted when Drym picked me up in the woods that night. I shrank from every man I needed to interact with, searching faces as I went about my day, scared to death I would see one of the men who held me.

Then I came home and felt safe because one seven-foot-tall monster slept in the maintenance room on my floor and another one watched obsessively from the oak tree outside my window.

It should have freaked me the fuck out. My brain should have felt scrambled and wrong. I should have felt ashamed every time I brought myself to orgasm thinking about a thick cock with a spiral of spikes down its length pushing into me.

I felt none of those things.

What made me feel weird was being out in the world. I hadn't needed to go back to work just yet, but my apartment felt empty and exposed. Walking down the sidewalk made me anxious. I was paranoid in the grocery store.

All I wanted to do was find a cave to hide in. One with a soft nest of blankets and a hot, furred body curled around me.

I shook my head. I wasn't sure what the future held for the wyrfangs, but I didn't see any way I fit into it.

I stepped back to let them in, chuckling when Quin's horns hit the top of the door frame and wrenched his head back. Drym shoved him the rest of the way through, ducking so he didn't repeat the mistake.

Quin rubbed at the base of his horns and shrugged at me. "We usually breach doors on all fours."

I closed the door and turned to find Drym close, staring down at me. I saw his hands wave at his side, like he wanted to reach for me, but decided against it. The slight movement broke my heart.

I stepped into him and dug my fingers into the fur on his back. My cheek pressed to his chest muffled my voice when I said, "Hi."

I felt the underside of his jaw press against my back and heard him whisper back. "Hi."

It started as a simple hug. I inhaled deeply and my nipples rubbed against his chest through the fabric of the thin cotton shirt I was wearing and heat flooded my body. My arousal was swift and so complete, I could feel how wet I was when I squeezed my thighs together.

A low rumble started beneath my ear and I knew he could smell how turned on I was.

Quin cleared his throat and I jerked away from Drym. I'd forgotten we weren't alone.

I cleared my throat and willed the heat out of my cheeks. "Are y'all hungry? Thirsty?"

Quin laughed. "I'm sure my brother is hungry, but he's going to have to wait. Right now, I need to satisfy my curiosity about what's in that note."

Oh, right. The note. The envelope was thin and sealed with an embossed circle of gold foil. I pulled out a single sheet of paper that was so smooth I knew it was expensive. There was no message, just a time and an address near the river.

I crossed to my couch and grabbed my laptop. There wasn't a business name associated with the address, but the satellite image showed a brick building with manicured landscaping in a fancy part of downtown Damruck.

Setting the meeting at eight at night meant as long as there were no floodlights on the outside of the building, Drym and Kragen could go with me. I just had to figure out how to get them there without being spotted.

Their size was an issue, but I'd seen Drym squat and tuck himself into a ball that made him seem far smaller. The horns were harder to hide.

"Okay, here's the plan. I want Drym to go with me, and I'm sure Kragen wants to go as well." I paused to make sure they were both following along.

Quin sank to the floor and tipped his nose skyward. "Thank fuck you didn't say me."

I snorted, then kept going. "Quin, you go back and tell Kragen to meet us at seven near the edge of the parking lot tomorrow. I'll go in the morning and rent a van big enough to hide you." I looked at Drym. "When we get to the address, it'll be up to you and him to figure out how to get inside."

"Good plan."

Drym's praise lifted my chest and I refused to examine that too closely.

"We better go before it gets too light out."

Quin stepped through the door but when Drym tried to follow, I stopped him. "Stay. Please."

He and Quin shared a look before the other wyrfang closed the door behind him with a soft click.

I watched Drym's shoulders rise and fall with a deep breath. "This may not be wise. I don't want to encroach on your space. I should go."

When he reached for the door handle I stopped him again. "Don't. I want you to stay." I took a deep breath of my own. "I want you."

KENZIE KELLY

TEN

I SPUN AROUND SO fast my tail whacked the door. "I can't keep from touching you."

Her hand reached out and trailed down my chest. "I don't want you to."

The growl that erupted from me was primal. I dropped to my haunches in front of her and stared into her eyes as I lifted her shirt from her body. My need to bare her skin warred with the need to make sure she wanted what I was doing.

She lifted her arms, making it easier to get rid of the shirt. I hooked my claws into the waistband of the pajama pants she was wearing, never breaking eye contact. She swayed toward me and her nipple brushed my nose. We both gasped.

My tongue flicked out, both halves curling around the hard nub and tugging. The scent of her, warm, earthy, and sweet, burned into me as I tasted her skin.

Her hands covered the backs of my fingers where they were hooked into her waistband and she pushed. Her pants fell in a puddle at her feet. Her underwear did nothing to diminish the honeysuckle smell of her arousal as it wrapped around me. My claws hooked into the sides of her panties, mindful of her soft skin. With barely a tug, I parted the fabric and it floated to the floor.

She wasn't a witch, but her scent, her taste, the little noises she made as I licked her, were a magic all their own. One that bound me tighter and tighter to her. I switched my tongue to the other nipple and she rocked toward me when I pulled the tight bud. Her hands gripped my shoulders for balance, and her back bowed, pressing her chest closer.

Heat rolled in my belly and I stiffened the sides of my slit, forcing my cock to stay hidden a while longer. My ass was rock hard, my tail twitching with the effort, but I was determined to see only to her pleasure.

I trailed my tongue down her abdomen, flicking at her belly button. I paused, my nose just brushing the curls at the juncture of her thighs.

"Please," she moaned on a whispered breath.

"Do you want me to lick you here?" I asked, my eyes closing as a fresh wave of arousal went through her.

"Yes."

My tongue shot out and dragged through her folds, lingering to tease her clit with a bit of pressure. I opened my mouth wider and shoved into her tight cunt, groaning as it sucked and squeezed me in welcome.

The blood rushed to my dick so fast I had no hope of keeping it contained. I wrapped my hands around the globes of her ass and pulled her closer, forcing her legs to either side of mine, her entire weight supported by my hands.

She grabbed my horns and moaned as her orgasm hit. I damn near came myself. I lapped at her until her breath returned to normal and every bit of her was clean. I gathered her into my arms as I stood and carried her to her bed.

I meant to leave her and sleep on the floor outside her bedroom door. Kendal was having none of it. When I tried to get up, she grabbed my cock and squeezed. I hissed as the pain and pleasure caused me to thrust into her fist.

"Where do you think you're going?" Her husky, sex-filled voice made me moan.

"You should rest." I tried to pull away but she held tight, stretching my skin to the point of pain.

"I'm tired of being told what to do. Tonight, right here, right now, I'm in charge."

I whimpered as pre cum leaked from my tip, the pleasure so intense my eyes rolled into my head. I was sure if she let go, I would come harder than I ever had. "I am yours to command."

She let go so fast I startled. On her knees, facing me in the bed, she was stunning. Fierce determination was etched into every line of her face. She looked like a warrior queen.

"Lie down on your back."

I was swift to comply. My horns kept my head bent at an angle that was perfect for watching her. She straddled my hips and I watched, fascinated, as her hand slid down her body, spearing into her folds and spreading them wide.

I reached for her, and she swatted me away with her other hand.

"No touching."

I growled and sank my claws into the bed. I would give her the control she wanted, even if it killed me. I could die happy staring at her beautiful skin glowing in the light of the moon.

She scooted forward and settled my cock in the valley between her labia, wrapping her hand around them both to hold herself closed around me. Then she rocked forward and back, dragging herself along my hard length.

My spikes flicked at her clit and we both moaned. Her head tipped forward and her dark curls caressed my stomach as she moved. Her tits swayed and I couldn't help but to drag the back of my fingers down the side of one soft globe.

She began to jerk and twitch as she slid up and down and I knew she was close. I wrapped my tail around her ankle and slid it upward, stroking her leg in time to her strokes on my cock.

I let it wander higher still, prodding at her opening.

"Fuuuck, Drym. You feel so good."

She stopped and lifted herself higher over me and notched me to her core. Her eyes flew to mine.

"I need you inside me. Now."

I gripped her hips, careful not to hurt her with my claws, and shoved my hips up while pulling her down. I hissed when I bottomed out, my slit hitting the heat of her. I surged up and flipped us, holding her shoulders as I moved in and out of her.

"Harder. Faster."

Her breath on my chest urged me on, but I still held back. Then she bit me. I growled and surged forward, pushing my hips to burrow as deep as I could. "You like it rough, little one?" My teeth scraped at the shell of her ear.

"Yes. I want to feel you lose control."

She got what she wanted.

KENZIE KELLY

ELEVEN

DRYM GROWLED AND HIS pace increased. He pounded into me, the only thing keeping me from traveling from his thrusts were his hands caging my shoulders. I could feel him bottoming out, the swirl of spikes scraping my insides as he pushed himself into me at a relentless pace.

He was so big it was a wonder he didn't hurt me more than the pleasurable sting of my skin stretching around him. I gasped when he pulled out and spun me, yanking me onto my knees, my butt in the air.

My pussy quivered and shook, the loss of him acute as cool air rushed over my exposed flesh. I whimpered. "Please, Drym."

I almost came when his warm breath huffed over me.

"Your pussy is so sweet, so perfect."

His tongue dragged through my folds, dipped into me, and then continued upward, probing at my ass. I tried to pull away, but his hands on my hips pulled me roughly onto his tongue.

He pulled out of me and I heard him smack his lips. "You are sweet everywhere."

He gave me no time to be mortified. He slammed his cock back into me and the stretch made me sigh in relief.

"Yes!" I cried out as his hips worked, giving me three fast, hard strokes before two agonizingly slow ones. I was so turned on, so wet, my juices were running down my legs.

He ran his claws up my spine and grabbed the back of my neck. I moaned as another wave of pleasure rolled over me.

"I will never let another touch you."

"God, Drym, I'm so close. Please…" I wasn't even sure what I was asking. I was teetering on the edge and I needed release. I slid my hand toward my clit, but he caught it and held it above my head.

"You want to come?"

"Yes! I need it, Drym." I pressed my forehead into the mattress, trying to push myself onto him harder.

"Then say it."

"Say what?" I'd say anything at that point.

"That you understand any creature that touches you will die under my claws. That you know what it means to let a monster fuck you."

"I understand!" My frustration had me close to tears.

"I need you to really understand, Kendal. I am a monster created to be a weapon. I will eviscerate anyone who tries to hurt you."

I swallowed, my pussy flooding at his words. I should be disturbed by how hot I found the idea that he would kill for me. His movements slowed to an impossible crawl, making me feel every one of his spikes as it popped out and then back into me. On an exhaled whisper, I said, "I understand."

He seemed to be everywhere all at once, whipping my need higher than I thought possible. He let go of my neck and trailed the tips of his claws down my back, his tail slid itself up my belly and between my breasts, curling around one and squeezing.

He was touching me everywhere but where I desperately needed him. I was so frantic I barely registered his tail tweaking my nipple before it let go. Then he pushed the tip of it hard against my clit and I shattered.

My legs locked and my lungs seized. He grabbed my hair and pulled my head back, his tongue flicking inside my mouth. I felt the scrape of his canines on my cheek and the heat of his chest against my back.

When my orgasm waned, he rubbed that sinful tail of his in circles and kept me going. He didn't stop until I collapsed.

He roared his own release and I felt his slit swell, almost painful where it pressed against my ass. My muscles trembled with aftershocks, so spent and weak I couldn't move.

He arranged us on our sides and petted my hair and stomach, whispering what a good girl I was into my ear.

He pulled away, and I whimpered, but he was soon back with a wet cloth. He wiped carefully up my legs and through my sex, which sent more spasms through me. He laid down behind me and gathered me into his arms. His legs were curled behind mine, his tail draped over and around my stomach.

I usually felt claustrophobic when lovers wanted to cuddle after sex. They wanted to hold too tight, they were too hot, my need to move became unbearable.

Not with Drym. I burrowed deeper into the cage that was him around me.

I was almost asleep when he whispered above my head.

"Are you ... are you okay?"

I heard the worry in his voice. I tried to find the right words for what I wanted to say, but it took a while.

He whined. "I'm sorry."

I ran my fingers into the fur on his forearm. "It's okay. I'm okay."

HELD BY A MONSTER

His muscles flexed under my hand, and I heard the breath blow through his snout. "I have never been possessive. Not like Roul. Even when we were young he didn't like to share. It never bothered me. I have never had something I wouldn't gladly give to one of my brothers."

I didn't know what to say, so I stayed silent.

"You are different. I love my brothers, and it would pain me, but I would tear their limbs from their bodies if they tried to take you from me. I say that about people I love. With anyone else, I wouldn't hesitate a second."

His words should scare the shit out of me, but they didn't. My damn heart was actually swooning at the thought of him being murderous over me. That was fucked up, but at the moment, I didn't care.

"I am a monster, Kendal. If you were smart, you would run very far from me."

I rolled in his arms and looked up at him, but he held me so close all I could see was the underside of his jaw. I curled my hand around his muzzle and pulled his nose down so I could look him in the eyes. "Then I'm the dumbest person alive, because I want you right next to me."

His eyes closed and he shuddered.

I kissed the side of his snout and he ran his nose up the side of my neck, settling on top of my head. I yawned and rubbed my check across the velvet skin of his chest, marveling how soft the skin was and how hard the muscle beneath. "Sleep now. Big day tomorrow."

He gave me a brief squeeze and pulled a blanket over us both.

I slept better than I had in a year.

TWELVE

MY EARS WERE FLAT against my head, my feet planted in the doorway.

Kendal grunted with the effort of trying to move me, her hands wrapped around my wrist.

She laughed and rolled her eyes at me. "I can't believe you're being a baby about this." She let go and waved at my body, doing an extra circle over my slit. "We're filthy. Covered in cum. The fur around your slit is crusty, for Christ's sake!"

"I will brush it." I was being surly.

She laughed and shook her head. "Not gonna cut it. Get in the shower."

I whined but let her move me an inch when she went around and pushed on my back with all her might.

She gave up and sighed. "Why are you so afraid of a shower?"

I shuddered and hung my head. "We were not allowed to bathe ourselves."

"Oh, Drym." I felt her move and then her face peered up at me, her eyes glassy. "What did they do?"

I shook my head. "It doesn't matter."

She grabbed my nose, her grip fierce. "It matters. What was done to you was wrong. Traumatic. And if you don't talk about it, it will leave lasting scars." She smoothed her hands up the sides of my muzzle and cupped my ears. "It will never be okay, but talking about it will make it better."

She gave me a wry grin. "Trust me, my therapist tells me that every time I see her."

I swallowed. Maybe she was right. "They sprayed us with a hose. It was powerful, and the water stung. They would throw buckets of soap flakes on us. If we were good and soaped ourselves as well as they thought we should, they would rinse us immediately. If they thought we missed a spot, they would let the soap dry on our skin and fur and repeat the entire process."

I chanced a look at her. I needed to see her reaction, and at the same time, dreaded seeing disgust on her face.

Instead, I saw anger. "Those fuckers!"

She wrapped both of her small hands around one of mine and stared into my eyes. "Do you trust me?"

I shouldn't. My trust should be broken beyond repair after the laboratory. We were all still wary of outsiders and went to great lengths to keep our existence a secret.

"Yes." My voice was strong and sure. Maybe I was a fool, but I trusted her.

She slowly walked backward, stepping into the large square enclosure first. The room had filled with steam and my fur clung to my skin. My eyes flicked to the wall, where a steady stream of water flowed.

She directed my hand to her chest, flattening my palm against her breast. My fingers squeezed and she inhaled sharply. I focused on her, worried my claws had nicked her skin. As I watched, she slid my hand to her side and down to her hip, across her belly to the other hip.

Then she spread her legs. My mouth watered and I smacked my lips.

I flinched when the water hit my arm. I hadn't been aware that she had backed far enough into the shower to be completely under the spray.

She turned my fingers down and slid them between her folds. She walked further back, until she pressed against the wall. Her head thrown back, she moaned as she used my hand to pleasure herself.

The water was hitting my chest. It was warm and soft. Soothing, not painful. I watched the drops fall and lifted my other hand, running my fingers back and forth through the water.

She brought my hand from between her legs and rubbed my forearm. I realized she was washing me. The soap in her hand left bubbles behind. The shower filled with the scent of flowers.

I stood dumbfounded as she moved up my arm, across my chest and down my other arm. She pulled on my shoulders and I dropped to my haunches. She washed my face and neck, careful to shield my eyes from the soap. She even ran her soft fingers along the curves of my horns.

No part of me was left untouched. Not even under my tail or in the crease of my slit. My dick pushed against her hand but I kept control. Only because she was efficient in her movements and didn't linger longer than necessary. That both relieved and disappointed me.

She must have known because she chuckled. "We can play later."

She moved me this way and that under the spray, washing and rinsing every inch of me until my fur squeaked and my tail scales gleamed.

My fingers itched to give her the same treatment, but my claws were sharp and I had to stay mindful not to hurt her. I stared at them and growled. "I should pull out my claws."

She gasped. "Don't you dare! Why would you even say a thing like that?"

"I want to touch you, rub your skin, the way you can touch me."

She bit at her bottom lip and kissed my chest. "We can figure something out. Something that doesn't involve mutilating your body."

I chuffed. If she thought there was a way, I would give her time to research. But I wouldn't wait forever. If her way didn't work, there was always mine. I was certain Cavi could remove my claws.

She bathed herself. I marveled at her beauty. I couldn't believe this creature allowed me to touch her. By the time she finished, my cock strained behind my slit.

She turned and caught me pushing on my groin, trying to hold it in.

She laughed. "Later. I have to go rent a van, and then we need to get ready to go meet this mysterious representative."

She turned off the water and stepped out, wrapping a large cloth around her body. I stepped out after her and shook.

She squealed and threw her arms up, holding the cloth in front of her.

Heat suffused my skin when I realized what I'd done. The room was now sopping wet. I hung my head. "I'm sorry."

She just laughed and shook her head. "It's okay." She leaned toward me and smelled my chest.

I staggered back in confusion.

She grinned up at me. "You smell earthy and clean."

My brows drew down in further confusion. "What else would I smell like? You washed every part of me."

She giggled again. "I thought you might smell like wet dog."

I growled and she fled the room with a giggle.

THIRTEEN

I WAS GETTING FRUSTRATED, and not in the good way. I tapped my fingernails on the counter. The ancient clerk at the rental counter hunt-and-pecked each letter as she typed in my name.

"I have a reservation for a work van," I repeated for the third time. I tried to be kind to workers. I thought of it like a bit of good karma keeping me from having to work thankless jobs.

She smiled up at me. "Yes, ma'am. I see it here. Would you like to add additional insurance?"

"No, thank you." I didn't want overpriced insurance that covered the same things my reasonable policy handled. I just wanted the damn keys. It was four o'clock. Sunset was at seven and my nerves started to build.

If we wanted to get to the meeting on time, I needed to hurry this along.

"I'll need to make a copy of your driver's license."

She looked surprised when I yanked it from my pocket and slid it across the counter. She picked it up and nodded, turning toward the back wall and a copier that looked like it had seen better days during the Reagan era.

The machine whined and knocked and I heard every gear as it picked up a piece of paper from the tray. I had to hope the printer wasn't similarly hindered. At some point, she would need to print out the rental agreement.

My fingers went back to tapping. I darted my gaze outside, worrying my lip at the purples and oranges already lighting the sky.

When she returned to her computer I gave her my best nice-person pleading smile. "Can I help speed the process? My boss is a stickler for punctuality and he expects me by six."

"Umm," she looked around as if there was any possibility another worker was present, "I'm not supposed to do this, but you can go ahead and sign the agreement. I'll fill in the details later, and we'll skip the walk around if that's okay."

My grin grew. "That's perfect. Thank you so much."

She gave me a conspiratorial wink. "I've had bosses like that. Insist you follow the rules, but do whatever they please. It's frustrating, but a paycheck's a paycheck, ya know?"

I played along and grumbled, "I just wish they were bigger."

We shared a good-natured laugh and within ten minutes, I had the keys in hand and was climbing into a windowless van. I was a nervous driver, but it was a recent thing. My therapist thought it was the fact that I was grabbed in a parking lot while walking to my car.

I wondered if any of the wyrfangs could drive. I can't imagine the scientists would teach them. I giggled at the picture of Drym folded into a sedan. Yeah, that wouldn't work very well.

I'd have to buy a van like this.

What? No. I couldn't keep him. We were from different worlds. It's not like I could walk down the street holding his hand like a normal boyfriend. People would freak out. And there was still the threat of the company behind the scientists.

They wouldn't be truly safe until every one of the people responsible was in jail or dead. Tonight was the first step, and I hoped the supernatural community helped them. It would be harder if they didn't, but they wouldn't give up. Their lives depended on them rooting out every person associated with creating them.

I took a deep breath and relaxed my grip on the steering wheel. I tried to lower my shoulders, but I knew they'd creep back up in no time.

It was only a couple of blocks to my apartment building and a few miles to the building in downtown Damruck. I'd driven the roads hundreds of times. It was no big deal.

I backed into a parking space as close to the woods as I could, peeling my fingers from the steering wheel one at a time. I hopped out on shaky legs. As soon as I had both back doors pulled open wide, two blurs moved in my peripheral vision.

I squeaked and scrambled away, losing my balance when my foot hit the curb. I braced myself for hitting the ground, but it never happened. I was yanked into powerful arms and found myself in the back of the van opposite Kragen.

Drym's voice rumbled beneath my ear. "Are you okay?"

"I'm fine, you just startled me is all. You're so fast. You came out of nowhere."

"I'm sorry, Kendal, we didn't mean to frighten you." Kragen's ears flicked back and forth.

Both of them seemed on edge. "Really, it's okay. Are you nervous?"

Drym released me and I bent to walk to the front. Both of them shook their heads.

HELD BY A MONSTER

"It's a little confining in here." Drym's voice was soft, but there was an edge to it.

It hit me like a ton of bricks. How else were they transported than in vans like this one? "This is how they moved you, isn't it? Took you on missions?"

"Usually in cargo trucks. But the metal walls are similar enough."

"Right." I hurried into the driver's seat. "Get the back shut and we'll get there as quick as possible."

Worry for them overrode my anxiety and I was able to drive with competence. We arrived with a few minutes to spare, so I circled the block, scoping the best place to park. Kragen and Drym needed cover to make it from the van to the building without being seen.

I found an entrance to an underground parking deck at the back and eased up to the gate. A speaker crackled to life as I rolled the window down.

"This isn't public parking." The voice was deep and clearly annoyed.

I imagined that happened often.

"Right, I know. I have an appointment."

"There are spaces in the front of the building."

"My... um..." I wracked my brain for what to call them. I didn't think monsters would go over well. "Companions have a sensitive... uh... complexion."

I smacked my palm against my face. They didn't know I was bringing anyone with me. I hoped my dumb move blowing the surprise wouldn't bite us in the ass.

The pause from the speaker was so long I thought he would tell us to park in the front again. I was surprised when the metal gate rattled upward.

Near identical black SUVs filled most of the spaces. A few random other cars were neatly lined up on one side. I pulled the big van into a space near them, high five-ing myself when I got out and saw I did a decent job. Nobody would want to park on either side of me, but I was in the lines. Mostly.

I had my hand on the handle of the back door when a low voice made me gasp and whirl around.

Three big, intimidating men stood in front of me.

I guessed it was a universal thing that supernaturals could appear out of thin air.

FOURTEEN

THE PLAN WAS TO wait in the van until the last possible moment, and then join Kendal as she walked into the building.

As soon as I heard her gasp and smelled three unfamiliar scents I was out the door and in front of her, my hackles raised. Kragen was on my heels, taking a similar position on her other side.

"What the actual fuck?"

The creatures stepped back, pulling guns from wherever they'd been hidden. Seeing them put me on higher alert. I growled a low warning. Our hybrid DNA made us impervious to most weapons. Bullet wounds would heal, but they still hurt.

Before I knew what she was doing, Kendal slipped between us and marched toward the other three.

"Hey! Put that shit away. I was invited!"

The one in the middle cracked a smile. "So you were. Kendal McPherson, I presume?"

She crossed her arms over her chest and nodded. I didn't like her so close to them, so I snaked a hand around her waist and pulled her back. The creature kept speaking.

"My name is Reinar Hilbertson. I own Superhuman Security." He waved a hand around to indicate the building. "I'm also a werewolf. These are my colleagues," he swung his hand to his left, "Vital Benoit, werebear," his hand swung right, "and Alexi Makarovich, also a werebear. We most often go by our code names." He pointed to himself, then at each bear in turn. "Zeus, Behemoth, and Russia."

My ears pinned back to my head and my growl got louder. I shoved Kendal behind me despite her *humph* of protest.

Kragen moved in front of both of us, closing half the distance between us and the others. "Kragen and Drym, wyrfangs."

"Wyrfangs? I've never heard of your species."

Kragen dipped his head. "We're new."

The one called Behemoth cocked his head. "Crossbreed?"

"Created," Kragen answered.

The three gave each other shocked looks.

"Should I be worried for my people's safety?"

He was clever to ask.

"Not unless you plan to attack us. We seek only answers, not bloodshed."

"Right," the werewolf said. "I think we should take this upstairs where we can sit down."

He led us through a thick steel door and my anxiety ramped up. Kragen and I could probably break through it, but the effort would leave Kendal open to attack. I felt much better when we entered an open space.

One of the bears walked toward another metal door, but the wolf—clearly the leader—stopped him with a chuckle. He looked up at our horns. "I think it best if we took the stairs."

A series of steps swept in an arc and carried us to an upper level. The walls were made of an abundance of glass, and Kragen and I pressed ourselves against the one solid wall. The odds a human walking by would see us on the second floor were low, but not zero.

The were-creatures had moved into another glass room. This one contained a long table and large screens on two walls. When he noticed we hadn't followed, he turned.

"It's one way glass." He nodded toward the outside walls. "We can see out, but no one can see in. It's necessary when working with Society clients." He moved back into the room. "Please have a seat. I have many questions."

Kragen cautiously moved to the far end of the table and I followed, keeping Kendal behind me despite her snorts of protest. I managed to sit in the offered chair. It was plush and the back didn't reach the seat, giving me a place to put my tail. It rolled and I shoved my claws into the floor to anchor myself.

I pulled Kendal into my lap and curled around her as best I could.

Kragen followed suit and settled into the chair next to mine. "We have questions as well."

"Me too!" Kendal shouted, her voice muffled behind my arms.

The wolf looked at the bear on his right and said, "Maybe you should ask Gaelynn to come. Seeing how we protect all mates might make them feel more at ease."

"Mate?" Kendal's voice was high-pitched and she started pushing against me in earnest.

I relented and loosened my arms enough for her to poke her head out before she hurt herself.

I heard the bear mutter, "Fuck no," in response to his superior.

If even these creatures saw nothing but monsters when they looked at us, where did we belong? Would we be shunned by all societies, human and supernatural alike? We would survive, but Kendal didn't deserve a life like that.

Her voice snapped me back to the present.

"What do you mean, mate?"

Kragen snapped his teeth together, the clack getting her attention. "Perhaps your questions can wait?"

A flush crept up her cheeks. "Right, right. Sorry."

For a long moment, we merely stared at each other. I didn't see any hostility in their body language, and their scents were neutral, but the bear's reluctance to bring his female wore on my mind.

Kragen broke the silence. "You're the supernatural's representative, Reinar?"

"Call me Zeus, the others do. And yes, I'm the Society council representative for this region."

"Society council? You also represent human society?"

"Ah, no. Society includes all supernatural individuals. We call humans 'normals.'" He shrugged. "Terminology that's easier to say than 'supernatural individuals' each time, since our numbers are vast and our forms varied."

Kragen nodded. "I understand. This council acts as a governing body over our kind? Separate from the normal's government?"

"That's correct. Only…" He tilted his head and ran his fingers through his hair. "I've never heard of *your* kind. Wyrfang, you said?"

"I'm not surprised you haven't heard of us. Our number is small. We asked Kendal to inquire about other Society in the hopes you could help us."

Zeus was nodding. "I'll do my best. What is it you need help with?"

Anger waved from Kragen like an oppressive heat. I found my own joining it.

"Finding the remaining members of the company that created us. And destroying them."

FIFTEEN

SHOCK ROLLED OVER THE three men's faces. I had to remind myself they weren't human.

The boss, Zeus, recovered first. "I think you should start from the beginning."

I felt both Kragen and Drym stiffen. I hadn't known them long, but I'd spent enough time to know that talking about the lab and what happened during their escape wasn't something they enjoyed.

I reached out and laid my hand on Kragen's forearm. "I won't presume to speak for you, but if it would be easier for me to lay out the basics, I'm happy to do it."

Drym's arms squeezed around me, and Kragen visibly relaxed.

"Thank you, Kendal."

I nodded. "Interrupt me if I miss something or get important details wrong."

His nose dipped in acknowledgment.

I spent a moment struggling with Drym's arms to gain more freedom. I knew he was trying to protect me, but I didn't want to speak to these Society members while muffled behind a huge, furred forearm. I took a deep breath when he relented and dropped his hands to my hips.

"I guess I should introduce myself. As you assumed, I'm Kendal McPherson, and I met the wyrfangs when one of them helped me escape from a bad situation." I chuckled at my understatement. "I haven't known them long, but I can tell you they are honorable, but most of all, they are worthy of your help.

"The wyrfangs were created in a laboratory. They are a hybrid of werewolf and dragon DNA."

One of them gasped and one other stiffened. Zeus's face turned thunderous.

"It's illegal and unethical to combine Society DNA in such a manner."

"Yes, well," I waved at Kragen and Drym, "obviously it being illegal didn't stop them."

"The council would never condone such a thing." Zeus slashed his hands through the air as he spoke.

"That's good to know, but our existence is proof the council's reach isn't infinite," Kragen growled and then waved me to continue.

"They were created and raised to be weapons—an elite combat unit. They were kept in captivity and routinely tortured in the name of science or training." I shuddered. "I'll let you fill in the blanks on their trauma. Anything you imagine is probably better than what they endured."

"What is the name of this laboratory? Who are these people?"

I appreciated that Zeus looked like he would rip them apart if they were in front of him.

"The company name was BioSynth Defense Solutions, but if they're smart, they won't use it anymore. The brothers don't know who was in charge of the facility or the research. They always used proxies, but from the level of surveillance they talk about, I imagine the big wigs were always watching."

Zeus nodded. "Where is this lab? Do they know anyone who worked there?"

Kragen answered. "Gone. Only one employee survived—the one who helped us escape."

The bear who'd been asked to bring his mate bit out, "Good."

The others nodded. I relaxed when they didn't scream murder or look horrified so many died.

Zeus speared his fingers through his hair. "Kendal, you're right. If they're smart, they'll ditch the company name and start over. Some government entities aren't smart, though, so we'll begin our search there. I'll need to contact the council about this." He sighed and met their eyes.

"I'll be honest with you. This is a mess. The council will surely bring you into the fold, but I can't say what they'll do with you. Neither weres nor dragons possess native magic for you to learn to conceal your appearance, and since our existence remains largely a secret to normals, that's a concern.

"There are other, similarly challenged species who live in protected areas, so that's an option. There are also witches who might craft a glamour to hide you, but glamours don't alter height and even that will make you stand out among normals.

"Ideally you'll be given land nearby for a protected area, identities to use online, and bank accounts to get you started with whatever you need."

He waved a hand in front of him. "But that's a discussion for another time. The priority is finding the people behind BioSynth and making them pay."

Kragen shook his head. "We are more interested in ensuring they can't repeat their experiments than in revenge."

I felt Drym rumble behind me and Kragen smirked in his direction.

"Though the opportunity to exact vengeance wouldn't be rejected."

Zeus nodded. "I understand. Where are you staying now? How can I get in touch?"

I spoke before either of the wyrfangs could. "Through me. I don't think it's wise to reveal their location just yet. I imagine BioSynth spent a hefty amount of resources in their creation and training, and I seriously doubt they'll walk away without trying to get them back."

The werewolf nodded. "Good point. I'll need your contact information, then. We'll arrange further meetings and pass information through Kendal." He looked at Drym. "If that's acceptable to you?"

Drym seemed surprised they would ask. His long silence stretched before he finally responded.

"If any harm comes to her, you will regret it."

Zeus tilted his head. "There is a lot of Society history you aren't aware of, and we'll help fill that gap. Werewolves and dragons both historically have fated mates. The way you are with her makes me suspect she"—he nodded in my direction—

"is yours. One thing I can assure you of is that all of Society shifters see fated mates as sacred, and any of us would lay down our lives to protect them. Not just our own, mind you, but *any* shifter's fated mate. They are rare and precious. No harm will ever come to Kendal if we can prevent it."

Oh wow, that was seriously hot. Not only did I have my very own monster—not under my bed, but in it, thank you—but any of these other powerful beasts would protect me with their lives.

I couldn't help the grin that spread across my face. "I'd love to meet the other fated mates."

Reinar laughed, a great booming sound that echoed through the conference room. "God help us when Virginia and Gaelynn get hold of you."

SIXTEEN

THE RETURN TRIP TO Kendal's apartment parking lot was done in silence, each of us lost in our own thoughts. Kendal was my mate. It felt right, but I wanted to know more. Were fated mates bound together in some way? Could she reject me?

My chest twisted at the thought.

Beyond the issue of Kendal being my mate, there was the entirety of Society for my brothers and me to wrap our heads around. Even though Zeus seemed willing to accept us, would the larger supernatural community be as open? Zeus said there were others like us, who couldn't hide among humans, so at least there were precedents for our situation. That didn't ensure we'd be treated like those others.

We weren't natural. We were created. Even we knew that meant we'd be treated differently. We hadn't been formally educated about Society or normals, beyond being taught to read and write. I remembered the debate among the scientists on whether even that education was wise. In the end, they decided if we couldn't read or write, then our functionality as weapons diminished.

We couldn't very well infiltrate a facility if we couldn't read which door was the entrance and what exits existed.

What little history, culture and manners we'd learned were self-taught. We listened closely to our captors, and we watched. We shared our observations and that's how we built an education beyond the limits the scientists set.

Kendal parked the van at the edge of the forest and opened the back doors for us. Kragen didn't hesitate, disappearing into the dark woods. I tilted my snout to look into Kendal's eyes. "I want to stay with you."

I shifted from paw to paw, nervous while she thought. She didn't look away, and my heart swelled.

"I don't think that's wise."

My ears flattened. "Can I ask why?"

"Of course you can. You can always ask questions. There are two main reasons. The first is that I don't think you'll be happy cooped up in my apartment alone all day. I have to go back to work tomorrow, so you'd be alone most of the time. And the second reason is that I think your brothers need you.

Right now, everything is unsettled. Until there is a clear path forward for the wyrfangs, you should be together."

My entire head sank, the weight of the rejection not lessened by her sensible logic.

Her hand beneath my chin lifted my eyes to hers. "That's not to say I won't visit, or that you can't come here sometimes."

The world lifted and my eyes glowed bright. Given leave to visit, I could admit she was right. "Both of your reasons make perfect sense." I looked over my shoulder, spotting Kragen waiting patiently in the dark. "You know the way to the caves? For when the were-creatures contact you? Or should I come by each night?"

She smiled. "I know the way, but if you want to come by, I'll let you know when it's safe to come up."

I tipped my nose to her window. "How?"

"Umm," she thought a moment, "I'll turn the light on. The one next to the window. That will let you know it's okay to come inside."

I nodded and ran my nose up the side of her neck, paused for a fraction of a second, then turned and caught up with Kragen.

"Everything good?"

I nodded. "Everything is fine."

He grunted in response. "Good, because I need my second. Even though we don't know how Society will react, or what they might rule in our case, we need a plan. I don't want to wait for their decision to track BioSynth."

"Neither do I. We have the laptops from the lab. We can start combing through the data and compiling any information we find."

He nodded. "That's a good start, but we need to loop into a wider network."

I tapped a claw against my snout. "Kendal might know a way. I'll return tomorrow night and ask for her help."

We were almost at the cave entrance when I stopped him. "I need to find the men who took her, and make sure they never hurt her again."

Kragen licked his snout. "We'll consider them a trial run for taking on the rest of BioSynth. It will be good to go on a hunt of our own choosing."

We waited until we'd entered the main cavern and were surrounded by our brothers to lay out our initial plans. Ever the leader, Kragen immediately took control.

"We met three supernatural creatures tonight, and their leader agreed to help us. He will take our case to the governing council and report back through Kendal. While we wait, we will move forward with two primary objectives. The first is finding the men who held Kendal captive. Drym will lead this effort and when he has a working plan in place, we will use those men as a trial hunt.

"The second is finding what remains of BioSynth and ensuring the wyrfang data is destroyed. Cavi and Quin, you will help me go through the laptops we took and organize what we find. Roul and Thurl, you will get us ready for the initial hunt. Outfit us in gear as you see fit. We'll help with resources as we find them."

He paused, his gold eyes sweeping over each of us. "Does anyone have anything to add at this point?"

Our brothers shook their heads.

"Good. Then let's get these fuckers and ensure they can't do this again."

I joined the chorus of howls that echoed through the caves.

I GRABBED MY horns and let out a grunt of frustration. I never appreciated how complicated the human world could be. It seemed so easy when the scientists brought them a file with target information. The address, entrances, exits, and weaknesses and strengths all laid out for them in neatly typed pages.

I'd gone to the mansion where they held Kendal, hoping to find the names of the men who'd hunted her. I searched the entire house, top to bottom, and came up empty. The house was simply a staging ground. No personal pictures on the walls, all the decorative touches generic. The only room that seemed used was one that housed several leather chairs and a large fireplace.

A display above the mantle held a rack of guns, and a bar with gleaming crystal glasses and various decanters of alcohol stood to the side.

The chairs were worn smooth where a man would sit, testifying to their extended use.

Other than that, the house was clean. Sterile. No papers in the drawers of desks, no drawer filled with random items. I even walked the winding driveway to check the mailbox. Empty.

The last area I searched was the basement. Rage coursed through my blood as I stood in the middle of the cages. Cages where Kendal and other women had been kept like animals.

Like we'd been kept.

The metal bars were no match for my strength. I ripped the doors off their hinges. In contrast to the upstairs, each of these cells held mementos. I carefully gathered what I found. Kendal would want to contact anyone who might miss these women.

I knew they'd had no family, but there might be friends, coworkers, someone.

If nothing else, I would remember them.

A locket with the picture of a smiling woman inside. A hair clip that sparkled in the dim light. A heart-shaped stone, worn smooth in the middle. A coin, one edge worn from being used to scrape lines in the stone wall.

A small bag held the treasures of these women as I made my way back to the caves. Every step increased my anger, the fog pushing at the edges of my vision. I took a deep breath and counted to ten as I exhaled. Losing myself wouldn't help Kendal.

Her soft curves and intoxicating scent filled my mind. At the last minute I cut right, skirting the cave entrance and heading toward her apartment. It was late, and I hadn't meant to come so soon, but I couldn't stop my paws from turning in her direction.

I stared at the ground for a long time before gathering the courage to look up. I wanted the light to be on. I wanted her to invite me in. My eyes scaled the beige brick of the building an inch at a time until the glow from the window snapped them upwards.

I started for the door, only to retreat when a laughing couple pushed their way outside. I thought I'd wait until they got into their car and drove off, but they stood beside it kissing for so long I said fuck it and slipped past. They were too caught up in each other to notice me.

I knocked on Kendal's door as gently as I could, but the sound still echoed through the hall. Three locks turned before the door swung open and she launched herself into my arms. I curled my body around her, backing her into the room before a flick of my tail shut the door.

Her hands fisted in the fur at my back and she pressed her nose to my chest, inhaling. My cock threatened behind my seam, but I managed to keep it contained. "Shh, you're safe. I've got you."

She nodded, but didn't let go or ease her grip.

"What happened?"

She shook her head so I lifted her and crossed to the couch. I settled her on my lap, guiding her legs to the sides of my hips. She pressed closer, as if she needed to crawl beneath my fur.

We sat like that for a long time until finally, her fingers eased and she sat back to look up at me.

"I went back to work today."

My arms squeezed her in encouragement.

"I thought I would be fine. I felt strong, confident. Then my coworkers kept asking how I was, what happened. Every time they asked a question, images flashed through my mind. The other women, the sound of the men shouting, the dogs barking."

I rested my lower jaw against her back and hugged her to me.

She shivered. "I started thinking things… paranoid things. They were just curious, maybe even a little concerned for me, but it was like being on high alert all day. It was exhausting. All I could think about was coming back here, switching the lamp on, and hoping against hope you'd see the light and hold me."

"I'm never far. You can always come to me."

"I know, but …" she turned her face away, her eyes at the floor. She whispered, "I'm afraid to go into the woods."

I tucked my claw into my palm and lifted her chin with the flat of my finger. "It's a reasonable fear."

"You have your own issues to deal with, you and your brothers. I hate to ask anything more of you."

"Ask for the world, Kendal, and I will give it to you." My heart cracked when she looked at me. Her eyes swam with tears and she blinked rapidly before they spilled down her cheek.

"Will you come every night? Maybe one day I will be brave enough to leave the light off, but until then, can you come?"

I ran my fingers through the silken strands of her hair, watching the light play in the dark strands. I wanted to tell her I couldn't stay away. I wanted to tell her I loved her, but I knew it was too soon. I needed to wait for her. To move at her pace. "Yes. I will come every night."

She sighed and relaxed into my arms, and it felt like heaven.

SEVENTEEN

AFTER SEVERAL MINUTES OF being held, I worked up the courage to ask him, "How do you not have nightmares?"

"Who said I don't?"

"Then how do you cope with them? The only time I feel safe is when I'm in your arms. I couldn't focus at all today at work. I kept looking around, waiting for someone to snatch me from my cubicle. To tell me my escape was just a dream and that I was still trapped in that basement."

His arms tightened around me and I burrowed deeper into his chest.

"We might have had an easier time because until very recently we didn't know there was any other way to exist. Our whole lives were spent in captivity, our every move dictated by the whims of scientists and militants.

"It's only since escaping that we've experienced kindness and comfort."

I sat up and speared my fingers into his ruff, then smoothed my palms over his ears. "When I think of what you must have gone through, my own experience pales in comparison."

He shook his head. "No. Your trauma is no less traumatic."

He buried his nose in my hair and we sat in the quiet for several minutes.

"Would it help to tell me what happened?"

I snorted. "My therapist wants me to open up about it. She says that talking about it out loud will make it more concrete, and less like a bogeyman. That it will help me move on."

"Do you believe her?"

I sucked in a breath. In a small voice I answered, "I do."

"Would you tell me? I've been told I'm a good listener."

There was a certain vulnerability in the way he asked. Like he wanted me to trust him with my demons, but he also didn't want to push too hard. It cracked my heart wide open, and all my trauma and fear came pouring out.

"I was walking to my car after work and a van pulled up next to me. I didn't think anything of it at first. It's a public parking lot so strange cars are often parked there. I only looked over when I heard the side door open.

"Two men jumped out. They had masks and gloves on. I remember thinking I had to fight, but I never got the chance. They were too strong. Something was shoved against my face and everything went dark."

I swallowed hard. I think if Drym had made the tiniest sound, I wouldn't have been able to continue. But he didn't.

"When I woke up, I was in the basement. The others—Sarah, Grace, and Catherine—were standing in their cages staring at me. Catherine was quiet. She'd been there the longest. Grace greeted me with a smile and said, 'Welcome to hell!' in a cheery voice even as tears streaked down her face.

"I asked them what was going on, but before they could answer three men walked in. Two of them were obviously powerful. They walked like they owned the world. The third carried a clipboard and took notes as the other two spoke.

"They were…"

I choked on a sob, and Drym's arms tightened around me.

"They were giving us numbers. I didn't realize until later it was the order they'd hunt us. Catherine knew. She pressed herself against the bars and spit at them, hurled curses and even reached an arm through to try and grab them.

"Sarah cowered in the back of her cell, her knees tucked to her chest and her head down." I shook my head. "She presented no challenge. That's what they said about her."

Drym's hand smoothed up and down my back and I tried to relax my shoulders and fists.

"They took her first. I kept thinking they were just going to rape her, and she'd be back. That we'd work out a way to escape together.

"They took Grace three days later. She walked out with her head held high. I don't think she played their game. We could hear the dogs just outside. Could hear her screaming at them, saying she refused to run."

I took a deep breath.

"The crack of the gunshot was so loud."

I swiped my wet cheeks on Drym's chest.

"After that, they told us the rules of the game. If we made it to the perimeter of their hunting area, we'd be free. Neither of us thought that was true. Catherine flat out told them it was bullshit, but they insisted. Told us the perimeter was marked with plastic tape tied around trees.

"We both knew they didn't want a repeat of Grace. It was no fun for them if we didn't run. What's a hunt where the prey gives up?" I snorted.

"That didn't mean I wasn't going to try. I expected to be next, but they took Catherine instead. Before she passed through the doorway she looked back at me. Determination was etched in every one of her muscles. We nodded at each other, and then she was gone.

"I think that was the worst part. Watching as one by one they were led out and never returned. Seeing our numbers dwindle and knowing there was nothing I could do to stop it.

"We tried. We dug at the window casings, but they were metal set into stone. We tried to lure the guards close enough to grab them. We tried to find anything we could use as a weapon.

"Every time a thought didn't work, or a plan failed, our hope dimmed. When they came to lead me out, I didn't look back. As soon as my feet hit the dirt outside, I took off. I ran as fast as I could, knowing I wouldn't be fast enough."

I wrapped my arms around Drym's neck.

"My mind knew it was hopeless, but my body wouldn't give up. I would be dead if it weren't for you. Some rich asshole's prize to brag about with other rich assholes."

"I am glad beyond measure that you found me, Kendal."

I looked into my monster's eyes and said, "Not nearly as glad as I am you found me."

DRYM KEPT HIS word. Every night that week, just after full dark, the gentle knock came at my door. Every night he held me, cradled in his arms. Never once did he push for more.

I still desired him. I'd felt his big, beautiful cock, and it ruined me for any other, but the stress of moving through the world all day kept our nights chaste. I prowled my apartment from the time I got home until I heard that scratch at the door. Restless, unable to settle until he arrived.

Only in his arms, surrounded by his body, could I sleep.

My therapist would not approve. I knew full well I'd moved into unhealthy territory. I didn't care. My coping mechanism may be bad, but who was I to say it wasn't exactly what I needed?

Somewhere in the far reaches of my mind, I knew a crash was coming. That was a problem for future me. Present me was blissfully ignorant of all issues that might arise from staunchly ignoring my mental health and relying on a seven-foot-tall monster security blanket.

I was more at ease with Drym than with any human I knew. The fourth night, he showed up with a laptop. He explained they'd purloined it from BioSynth. I offered to help him comb the data for information on who owned the company and where they might have run.

"My brothers are looking into that." He said from the other end of the couch.

My face scrunched in confusion. "So what are you looking for?"

He never looked up from tapping on the keyboard as he replied, "Your kidnappers."

I fell back onto the couch in shock. My eyes trained on him and the ridiculous sight he made. The laptop seemed tiny under his huge hands, his typing slow and careful as he pressed each key with a claw.

"Why are you looking for my kidnappers?"

His ears flicked back and forth, the end of his tail thumping on the wooden floor. "To kill them."

His voice held such malice, his expression determined as he continued to click the keys. Heat flooded through me. I saw his nose twitch before his glowing eyes raised to mine. I should be embarrassed that he smelled my arousal, but it just made me wetter.

My breath grew heavy as we stared at each other. I licked my lips and saw his eyes dart to them. I took a deep breath. "I need you."

He closed the laptop and carefully set it on the floor before turning toward me. "What do you need from me?"

I ignored the flush that rose on my skin and pushed past the embarrassment. How could I still be embarrassed? "I need you to fuck me."

He started and I saw his fingers flex. "How do you need me to fuck you?"

I tilted my head. "What do you mean?"

His nose lowered, his back hunched until he was staring straight into my eyes. "Do you need it slow and gentle, a rising crescendo that builds until you can't stand it anymore and you beg for release? Or do you need it hard and fast, with me pounding into you and using your body until it shatters beneath me?"

It was hard to push words from my panting chest. "Yes," was all I managed.

He nodded and somehow understood what I meant. My knees were bent, my back against the opposite arm of the couch. I jumped when his hands curled around my ankles and pulled, laying me flat on my back. My sleep shirt rode up my stomach, my shorts bunched around my waist.

He slid my shorts and underwear off my legs in one smooth pull. He spread my thighs, one foot on the floor and the other wrapped around his back. My gasp when his cold, wet nose trailed up my inner thigh turned into a moan as he attacked my clit with his forked tongue.

In seconds I was writhing beneath him, trying to push closer, riding his tongue with wanton abandon. His hands circled my hips, holding me in place as he feasted. Tension coiled and built and as suddenly as he'd started, he pulled away. I whimpered as cool air hit my flesh.

I felt his cock notched at my entrance and tried to lift my hips to greet him, but he held them still. He filled me in one smooth thrust, the spikes along his shaft scraping deliciously along my walls.

Seated to the hilt, he ground the growing bump at the top of his slit against my clit. He pulled out, thrust, circled his small knot on my clit again and again. He set a steady, punishing rhythm. Without his hands holding my hips, I would have traveled the length of the couch. Each time he withdrew, he pulled me toward him.

His teeth nipped at my neck, my chest, my breasts, his tongue flicking at my ear. He was everywhere at once, and dominated my body as he'd promised. I dug my fingers into the thick fur at his shoulders and bowed my back. His tail wrapped around my thigh and squeezed, pulling me impossibly wide. The angle of his thrusts changed and I moaned as he slid along the bundle of nerves, crashing into my cervix. His pace increased just to the point of pain. I was so turned on liquid rushed from me, making his thrusts squelch erotically.

"Come. Now," he demanded in my ear as his teeth rasped the space between my neck and shoulder.

My body obeyed and I screamed. The world seemed to go black, the only sensation him moving over and into my body. I drifted down, aftershocks making my legs jump.

He slid to the floor and sat me up on the couch, my legs forced wide by his body. I nearly came unglued when he swept his tongue up my cleft, circling my clit. I looked at him in shock through hooded lids.

"I'm not even close to done with you."

EIGHTEEN

I WASN'T SURE IF what I'd said was okay. "Unless you want me to stop?"

I would. She only had to say the word. I was more than happy to hold her close and listen to her breathe as she slept.

"No, don't stop."

I attacked her cunt like it was my salvation. It was, and it wasn't. Salvation was all of her. My heart thumped in my chest, my love for her swelling and invading every cell in my body. It was supposed to be irrational. I'd heard enough humans lament their relationships to know love wasn't supposed to develop that fast.

Listened enough to know if I said how I felt aloud, I would scare her. Terrify her.

It must be a function of the mate bond the shifter mentioned, but I didn't know enough about it to be sure.

She went through something incredibly traumatic. I would not add to that trauma. I wanted to be a source of safety. To be the one place her anxiety melted and was replaced by warm feelings.

Her channel quivered around my tongue and I flicked faster. I held her, spread wide before me, and watched as she orgasmed. Her thighs pushed against my shoulders, her ankle shaking where my tail held it. Her hands fisted the pillow under her neck and her back lifted as she shattered.

It was the most beautiful thing I had ever witnessed.

I wanted to watch her come again, and again, until her body was too exhausted to reach another peak.

I eased my tongue from her as the aftershocks subsided and licked her leg from where my tail held it up and over her belly and back to her neck. The urge to bite her overwhelmed my senses. My mouth watered and my teeth clicked together as I clamped my jaw shut.

I didn't know what that instinct was. I'd never felt it before. But something in me knew it was an irreversible step. One I could not take without her explicit consent.

I emptied my lungs through my nose and sat up, away from the temptation.

Her eyes traveled down my body, growing wide as they landed on my still erect, still straining cock.

"You didn't…?"

I shook my head, afraid if I opened my jaw to speak my teeth would fall on the soft spot between her neck and shoulder and draw blood.

She reached for me, her soft hand just brushing the head of my dick before I leaped away from her. My eyes rolled in my head and I shook myself out like I was wet.

"Tonight was for you."

She collapsed back on the couch, not as exhausted as I'd like to make her, but tired enough to not care she remained spreadeagle. Her right leg draped over the back of the couch, her left foot on the floor.

She shuddered a deep breath and I followed suit. After three more, her eyes finally blinked open. "Can you stay?"

I nodded and scooped her up. I carried her to the bed and arranged her on top of me, her head on my chest, most of her body cradled between my legs.

I watched her sleep, staying as still as possible. I ignored the cramps in my knees and ankles, the position on my back awkward for my anatomy.

The sun turned the sky a dusty pink and it was time to go. I packed up the laptop and the few things I'd taken from the kidnappers' house. I snuggled my muzzle into her hair, careful not to touch her skin with my cold nose.

She made a sleepy noise and turned toward me.

"Dawn approaches, little one. I have to go."

Her arms escaped the blanket I'd covered her with and wound around my neck.

"Be safe."

I chuckled. "I think I should be saying that to you."

She smiled without opening her eyes.

From the other room came the unmistakable sound of paper being slid under her door. My ears pricked and she released me, her eyes wide as she followed my gaze.

"What is it?" Her voice was barely a whisper.

"Stay here."

She nodded, but her entire body tensed. I hated her fear. It wasn't enough for me to kill the men who took her. She needed to know they were dead. That they would never hurt her again.

The door was still locked; the windows closed. Nothing was amiss. A piece of folded paper lay in the middle of the floor. I picked it up and carried it to her. I wanted to read it, to make sure it was friendly. A notice from her apartment manager, a takeout menu. I told myself it could be any of those things, but my gut said otherwise.

I still wouldn't read it before her. I grew up with no privacy. No way to escape the constantly watching eyes. Everything we did was on display.

This note was not meant for me, so unless she said otherwise I would not read it.

I held it out to her. "It was slipped under your door."

Her eyes flew to the doorway that led to the front door and back to me. "What do you think it is?"

She made no move to take it. I shrugged. "I don't know."

"You read it. It could be from the Society council."

My shoulders dropped a few inches and I exhaled before carefully unfolding the sheet of paper.

We have reason to believe the kidnappers haven't given up. Take every precaution with your safety. -Zeus

My fingers tensed, and my claws ripped through the paper.

Kendal gave a nervous chuckle. "That good?"

My vision fogged at the edges. "I don't want you to leave this apartment without me."

She bent her knees and wrapped her arms around her legs. "I have to work, Drym. I have bills to pay."

Her voice was thready and unnaturally high. My teeth ground together. "I know. Can you take a bit more time off?"

Just until I found and eviscerated those fuckers. I kept that to myself. She didn't need to know the contents of the message.

She knew it was bad from my reaction.

She nodded. "Another day or two, maybe."

"Will you come home with me?" She was safer in the caves, surrounded by my brothers.

Her throat bobbed as she swallowed. I knew she was thinking about walking into the still dark forest.

Her reluctant nod told me she was more afraid of what I wasn't telling her than the forest. My heart cracked. She shouldn't be afraid. She should never have to be afraid again.

I'd protect her. Even if it meant exposing myself to the world.

NINETEEN

MY HEART WAS POUNDING out of my chest but Drym gave me space to decide. Whatever that paper said, it had made him furious. His gold eyes took on a reddish cast, glowing so bright it was like twin flashlights in my darkened bedroom.

It had to be from my kidnappers. I was deathly afraid of walking into the dark forest again, but staying here was out of the question. They knew where I lived.

"Gather what you need for two days. Wait until it's full light. I'll keep watch from just inside the forest's edge and meet you when you get there."

He was risking exposure getting that close to being out in the open. Selfishly, I didn't care. I knew there was no way I'd be able to walk into those trees by myself. My throat felt like the Sahara. Or was it the Sonoran? Whichever place was drier.

I nodded.

"I will watch you every step of the way. I am fast enough to run down a vehicle. You will *not* be taken from me."

I inhaled and nodded again, still unable to form words.

He turned and left, his tail quivering at the tip in agitation.

He wasn't leaving me. He was going to wait. He'd meet me at the edge of the forest. I repeated the plan in my head until I packed a small bag with a few changes of clothes and toiletries. I wore my lightweight hiking boots. I wasn't a hiker, but I aspired to be one year. They had excellent traction, according to the person who sold them to me.

I wanted excellent traction if I needed to run.

I shook the thought from my head. I wouldn't need to run. Drym waited for me just inside the tree line.

I perched on the edge of the couch, staring out the window. The sky lightened through several shades of purple, red, and orange before finally settling into an overcast blue. I dialed my boss, told her I needed to take another couple of days off and she was sympathetic.

The last task taken care of, I guessed I had to pull up my big girl panties and get going. The sun wasn't going to help anymore today.

My head hunched into my shoulders, I speed walked across the parking lot. I almost made myself dizzy, darting my eyes back and forth, searching for threats. Twenty feet, nineteen, seventeen feet, then fifteen feet left between me and the tree line.

A shadow moved in the forest. Drym, swaying so my eyes could pick him out. Letting me know he was there.

Blood pounded in my ears, drowning out the sound of car doors opening behind me. Drym's eyes flashed red in the gloom and I heard him growl, "Run."

I didn't hesitate. I took off like a rocket, aimed at where he stood. Adrenaline made me faster than I'd ever been, but the pounding feet on the asphalt behind me seemed to get closer every second.

I reached Drym's arms and they folded around me, giving me a quick squeeze before he pushed me gently behind him. He looked over his shoulder at me. "Close your eyes, little one. Don't look. Don't move."

I knew he would never hurt me. I was certain he would make good on his promise to rip apart anyone who tried to take me from him. I closed my eyes.

The shift of air was the only indicator I had that he moved. I stood stock still. I heard the crunch of feet falling into the fallen leaves from last autumn, then a sliding noise and a scream cut impossibly short.

"What the fuck?"

I recognized that voice. That was one of the men who snatched me from the street. I squeezed my eyes shut and countered the impulse to open them. I held my bag to my chest, the strap cutting across my back.

Running footsteps from my left. "Bill! I found her!"

"No names, you fucking idiot!"

Now I knew his name was Bill. Fat lot of good that would do me. Why couldn't it be Moonbeam or something else unique?

Two sets of shuffling feet got closer. I kept my eyes shut tight, and other than uncontrolled trembling, planted my feet. The urge to run increased the closer the noises of the two men came, but I held my ground.

A small click proceeded a gurgle followed quickly by Bill saying, "Holy shiii—!"

The word cut off abruptly. A low howl pierced the silence. It was like the entire forest stopped to listen. The sound tapered off and Drym's voice, strong and soft, immediately followed.

"I want you to turn and face the opposite way."

My eyes fluttered.

"No, keep your eyes closed."

I nodded to let him know I understood and turned. Something from deep in the forest ran toward me. Something big and fast pushed through the underbrush. Every muscle in my body locked until I felt Drym's heat at my lower back.

"Quin is coming."

My head whipped to the side, but I kept my eyes closed. "Why?" I felt panic bubble in my chest. Why would Drym give me to Quin? Why wouldn't he take me himself?

"To carry the one I left alive."

"The other two?"

"Dead."

No emotion, no inflection in his voice. Just a simple fact.

"I want to see."

He stilled. I was thankful he didn't outright deny my request. However horrible the sight, I needed to see. To make my brain truly understand they couldn't come after me again.

"If you think it will help."

I nodded, took a deep breath, and opened my eyes. I was facing into the forest; the sunlight dappled where it hit the ground, a soft breeze rustling the branches high above. It was quiet. Tranquil even.

I turned around slowly.

One man was lying between two trees to my right. Or rather, his torso laid there. His head was several feet away. It looked like it had been torn from his body.

I felt ... nothing. No remorse, no regret. No nausea even. The only feeling I could summon was a hint of relief.

I swung my head to the left. One man was a crumpled lump on the ground. The one he'd left alive, I assumed, since he wasn't covered in blood or missing any limbs. The other's throat was gone. Not slit, not crushed, just gone. Like something grabbed it from the front and ripped it clean away.

No, not something. Drym.

I looked up into his eyes, now back to their normal gold color. He reached for me and then pulled back.

"Thank you." I let him see how much I meant those two words.

He reached for me again, and I took a step back. I smirked and waved at his arms. "You gotta take a bath before you touch me."

He started and looked down, staring at the blood and gore that soaked him from claw tip to bicep. He snorted. "Fine."

Quin slid to a stop in front of us and whistled. "Next time, leave some fun for the rest of us." He scanned me from head to toe. "You okay, Kendal?"

"I'm good. Do you mind guiding me to the caves? I think Drym should carry the one he left alive, because I'm not letting him carry me."

He laughed and bowed, extending his hand with a flourish. "It would be my pleasure."

Drym followed close behind, grumbling the entire way.

TWENTY

NONE OF US LIKED getting wet, so we'd never found or made a bathing area in the caves. I was really missing Kendal's shower as I plunged myself into the frigid lake on the far side of the forest.

I reminded myself holding Kendal was worth any discomfort.

I reentered the main room and found my brothers looming over our prisoner.

Roul started when he saw me. "You're wet."

I nodded. "I took a bath."

His jaw dropped and his ears flicked. "You took… a bath?"

I nodded and put my hand on his shoulder. "It's not so bad out here. Kendal showed me it can even feel good."

He stared at me like he wasn't sure he could believe me, but we'd never lied to each other. Roul snorted and pointed to the man, who was still out cold.

"How hard did you hit him, Drym?" Roul clicked his claws together. He was probably sadder than Quin to miss an opportunity to shed blood. He'd gone to a dark place after our escape, and nothing I nor my brothers did helped.

I leaned down into the man's face and saw a telltale flinch. "Not hard enough to keep him out this long. He's faking."

Before any of us could react, Roul slid his claws down the man's side leaving behind four neat trails of blood. The cuts were superficial, but they got the intended effect.

He jerked against the ropes holding him with a hissed, "Fuck!"

Roul leaned back and crossed his arms over his chest. "Better to face the beasts than hide, idiot."

Kragen tilted his head. "So, Bill…"

The man's—Bill's, apparently—skin drained of color, his saucer eyes stuck on Kragen's jaw. "You're … real?" The simple words strangled out of him.

Kendal pushed herself between me and Kragen and stood her ground despite my best efforts to shove her back.

"What, you thought they were men in fursuits or something?" She rolled her eyes. "You're smart enough to snatch women off the street with no one noticing, but you didn't figure that out? Didn't you see your friend get ripped in half?"

"I thought ... masks ... blades..."

"Swords only slice through people in movies, dumbass. Unless you're talking a two-handed broadsword and that was more of a"—she flattened her hand and dropped it from shoulder height—"downward swing type thing."

Bill wasn't the only one looking askance at her.

She shrugged. "I went through a sword phase."

I turned my attention back to Bill. "Now that our existence is cleared up, can we get on with it?" I cocked an eyebrow at Kragen.

Quin bounced on his paws. "I don't know. It's kind of amusing to see a normal learn of our existence. I thought there'd be more screaming and running, though."

Thurl punched him in the shoulder. "Where is he going to run, dumbass? We're in a cave. And he was unconscious until a minute ago. I'm sure the screaming would have happened if he knew from the get go that we were real."

"I can scream if you want me to."

A surge of anger hit me. He was already entering the bargaining phase, which meant I wouldn't get to hurt him as much as I wanted. This man had hunted Kendal. Scared her. *Put his hands on her.* I wanted to make him suffer before he died.

"He was at the house?" I ran the back of a finger down Kendal's soft cheek. I wasn't sure if I was grounding her or myself.

"Yeah. He was one of the ones who took me. Then he was one of the regular ones who brought us food and water in the basement."

I growled and my arm drew back, determined to mimic Roul's earlier move only deeper and aimed at his neck.

Kragen caught my wrist before I could connect.

"Answers first, brother."

Three shaky inhales later I was able to step back. Kendal wrapped her right arm around my waist and her scent settled me. I did my best to ignore Bill and shoved my nose into her hair.

"What are the names of the men who were present at the house?" Cavi took over the questioning from where he stood at the long table, an open laptop in front of him.

Bill shook his head. "I don't know."

"Bullshit!" Kendal spit.

His eyes big as saucers, Bill scanned the monsters surrounding him. "I swear! I didn't ask questions."

"How were you paid?" Kragen moved to stand in front of him.

"In cash. Look, they were careful and paranoid. They never used real names, only code names. Always wore masks while the hired help was around. Never arrived in the same car, never brought anything personal with them."

"That's a lot of detail for someone who never asked questions." Roul snapped his teeth close to Bill's neck.

A dark stain bloomed over the man's crotch. The smell of urine flooded the cavern. I dragged Kendal back a step in disgust.

"Me and Sam——." Bill swallowed hard.

I surmised Sam was one of the bodies we left in the woods.

"We'd been casing them for months. They had to be rich, right? Never showing up in the same car, with expensive gear and fancy guns. We thought if we could get a bead on even one of them, we'd be set for life. Nobody that fancy would want their side hobby going public."

"You mentioned code names?" Cavi tapped away on the laptop, taking notes. He was the fastest of us at typing, but he was still slow.

Kendal slipped under my arm and pushed him aside to take his place. Her fingers flew over the keys and in seconds she narrowed her eyes at Bill. "Code names, Bill."

He jumped and tried to turn to see her, but she was too far behind him. "Colors and numbers. I think the colors were the founding members, and the numbers came in later. They were talking about another round of guys, referring to them as letters."

"List the colors first." Kragen crouched in front of the man, his voice calm.

Bill nodded. "Yeah, yeah. There was Mr. Red, Mr. Blue, and Mr. Yellow."

Kendal paused her typing and I looked to make sure she was okay. Her head was tilted and her eyes wide.

"Primary colors."

Bill was nodding. "Yeah! That's why Sam and me figured they were the first."

"And the numbers?" Kragen asked.

"Misters one through five." He didn't wait to be prompted for the next list. "I only heard them talking about the letters once, but they were arguing about letting Mr. E join. Sounded like most of them didn't like him."

"Thank you, Bill." Kragen stood and flicked a knife from the man's boot. He spun it in his palm before offering it, hilt first, to Kendal.

TWENTY-ONE

I STARED AT THE blade, my brain taking way too long to figure out why Kragen was offering me a knife. The wyrfangs didn't need knives.

When it hit me, I didn't hesitate. I watched Bill as he tracked me grab the knife and move to stand in front of him. "This is for Sarah." I plunged the knife into his side. "This is for Grace." I stuck the knife into the top of his thigh.

His violent jerks against the ropes holding him caused the chair to rock back and forth. Drym stepped forward and put a massive hand on his shoulder, ceasing all movement. His eyes rolled and he wailed until his head slumped forward.

Roul flicked a claw through Bill's ear. "No passing out."

Bill whimpered.

"This is for Catherine." I shoved the blade into his belly. "And this is for me." The knife handle was slick with blood so I wiped my palm on Bill's pants before thrusting it into his chest. I pulled it back out and watched blood run from the wounds I'd inflicted. A sizable puddle formed on the floor.

Every time Bill passed out, one of the wyrfangs would slice a claw into his body until even that no longer roused him.

Drym's hand ran down my forearm and gently pried the knife from my fingers. "I'll get rid of these." He waved the knife to include Bill.

"Actually, I'd like to keep it." The six beasts went still. "The knife, I mean. Definitely get rid of the body."

I chuckled at the chorus of sighs. They would have let Bill rot in that cave if I wanted it, but I wasn't a masochist and the smell of blood was already overwhelming. I didn't need decomposition added on top.

Roul grabbed the back of Bill's chair and dragged it, and him, from the room.

I stood in the middle of the cavern, watching Bill's body until it disappeared into darkness. I could feel Drym standing behind me. I spun and stared up at him as tears gathered in my eyes. What had I done?

"I just killed a man in cold blood."

Drym nodded and took my hands in his. "You did."

I blinked and tears tracked down my cheeks. "Am I a monster? Am I like those men who hunted me for sport?"

He crouched in front of me, his eyes glowing bright gold rimmed with red. "Do you think me a monster?"

I shook my head. "No. The people who held you captive are the monsters."

"Then you are no more monster than I am, Kendal. I killed those men in the forest because they held you captive. I would have killed Bill for the same reason."

He stood and pulled me into a tight hug. I rubbed my check on the soft fur on his chest and sighed.

"Do you regret taking the knife?"

I thought about it for a long time as his warm palm slid soothing circles on my back. Did I regret taking the knife from Kragen? I could have just as easily stood by and watched one of the wyrfangs kill him. I didn't have to get so involved.

Catherine's face floated through my memory, fierce determination in her stiff posture as they led her from the basement. A memory of Grace, sobbing and begging to be let go morphed to one of Sarah, her small voice and timid movements etched into my brain. "No. He was part of the others being killed. I'm the only one left who can stand for them. They would have wanted me to do it. To take back a little of the power they took from all of us."

The rough timber of his voice vibrated through his chest. "Good girl." He pushed me to arm's length and then tipped my chin up with a finger. "Let's get you cleaned up."

I was confused until I saw my hand covered in blood, and more spattered across my shirt and pants. I shuddered and let him lead me to his nest where I found my bag and a basin of water. I scrubbed at my hands until I felt clean, emotionally washing away some of the trauma from earlier.

My therapist would have a field day with this.

I changed my clothes and balled up the bloody shirt and pants. Drym waited just outside the entrance to lead me back to the main area, where the other five wyrfangs were engaged in a heated debate. Roul and Thurl wanted to return to the house, certain the men wouldn't abandon such a prime location.

Kragen argued that there were too many variables, chief of which was time. They couldn't afford to be out in the open for the days or even weeks it might take for the men to return.

They all fell silent when I stepped up. "Kragen's right. You can't expose yourself like that for me." Several growls filled the air until I held up a hand. "We can still look for them. I think property records are public. I can start there while y'all work on finding more about the director of BioSynth."

"Kendal, they tried to take you again, in broad daylight." Drym's snarl elicited nodding from Roul and Thurl.

HELD BY A MONSTER

I put my hand on his chest, needing to touch him. "It will take them time to find new goons willing to do their dirty work. We have time."

"What if those weren't their only 'goons', as you call them?"

"Then we'll deal with them." The ever-present growl in the cavern reached a new volume. I looked at each wyrfang, making sure I had their attention. "I won't be alone. I'll be with you." I chuckled. "And with six monster bodyguards, I feel invincible."

"You will not go anywhere without one of us acting as your shadow." Drym shifted on his feet, clearly uncomfortable with the arrangement.

"I won't. I don't have a death wish, and I'm well aware they're too angry to let me loose on another hunt." I sighed. "Besides, they'll have learned what happened to the goons in the woods. They can't think I'm still easy prey."

They seemed to relax a bit, but Drym remained worried. I snuggled into his chest and hugged him tight. When I let go, I looked into his eyes and smiled. "Let's get to work."

TWENTY-TWO

I WAS NOT HAPPY to put off the search for Kendal's pursuers, but I had to admit, it made sense. As the day waned into night, I could relax. Seeing her tapping away on one of the stolen laptops, smiling and joking with my brothers, gave me a sense of peace I'd never experienced before.

It felt late when she slammed the lid of the laptop. The others startled and she waved a hand. "Sorry, I'm just getting frustrated. My searches are going nowhere." She rubbed at her eyes. "I think I need to call it a night. We can start fresh in the morning."

"Yes, you should rest." I moved to her. I couldn't touch her enough. I needed to have physical contact with her as much as possible. I didn't understand this compulsion, but it was no hardship to indulge it.

As we walked to my nest, she sighed and leaned into my side. "I think we need to check my apartment, and if there's no note from Superhuman Security, we should reach out again."

I nodded. "Okay." I wasn't sure we could trust the shifters, but time was the only solution to my fears. The more interactions we had with them, the better I could judge them.

My focus had shifted since our escape. I had been determined to find and destroy those in charge of BioSynth, aligned with my brothers in that task. Now, that seemed a secondary priority. Still important, logically, but my heart concentrated on Kendal. Making sure she was safe was paramount.

Our post-lab education was swift but there was one thing we'd learned that seemed to underpin everything. You needed currency to acquire goods and services. Jobs provided that currency to normals, but that was beyond our capabilities. The shifters mentioned others who were unable to integrate with normals being taken care of by Society.

I wondered if that extended to such creature's mates.

If Kendal didn't have to work, then I could always be by her side. Nothing could harm her as long as I was there.

She was right. We needed more information from the shifters. If they hadn't reached out, we needed to seek them out again.

My curiosity had grown about supernatural Society as well. Surely they had some sort of information repository—some way of sharing knowledge through generations.

Lost in my thoughts, I'd missed Kendal getting ready for bed. I must have made a noise of disappointment, because she giggled and patted the nest next to her.

"Come lie down with me until I fall asleep. I know you won't stay, y'all seem to need very little sleep and you'll want to go back and help. But I'd like you to hold me for a bit."

"I would stay if you ask me."

She gave me a sleepy smile. "I won't. You should help."

I curled myself around her, tucking her against my chest. It was like a great cog shifting into place. Her scent in my nose, her skin touching mine. It was a panacea for my soul. The world was right with her in my arms.

It frightened me.

The power she had over me was absolute. The very idea of losing her caused great pain. I wasn't sure I'd survive it.

I was determined not to let that happen.

I took a deep breath, filling my lungs with the smell of her warm skin. Her breathing was even and steady, so I carefully covered her with a blanket and slid from my room.

I found my brothers arguing again. Kragen held up a hand as I entered.

"Let's get Drym's opinion."

The others nodded. None of them looked happy.

"We need more information," Kragen began. "We are out of our depth navigating the outside world. We thought it would be simple enough to track the remaining BioSynth employees, but they kept us in the dark on technology and navigating the wider world."

He sighed. "Kendal's help is invaluable, but her knowledge doesn't extend as far as we need."

I nodded. "We discussed this before she fell asleep. She wants to check her apartment. If the shifters have reached out, we can ask for further assistance. If they haven't, we need to contact them."

"That's the central issue." Kragen pointed at Cavi, Roul and Thurl. "They don't trust them, and think we should continue on our own."

"I'm not sure I trust them either, but the only way to resolve our fears is to interact with them more. If at any point we deem them a threat, or untrustworthy, then we can sever our relationship. I see no harm in giving them a chance, granted we keep as much as possible to ourselves." I scratched at my bicep. "It will be a tricky thing, revealing enough for them to help without giving them the means to entrap us, but I think we can do it."

We stood, each silently assessing our options for several minutes. Roul suddenly threw his hands in the air. "Fine! We move forward with the shifters. But at the first sign of trouble, we burn them all."

There were a few noises of agreement, but we weren't ready to condemn them without cause. That was good. It meant that even the more suspicious among us saw the value in getting the help we needed.

The only question that remained was whether they would share the level of information we sought.

We'd learn that answer soon enough.

KENZIE KELLY

TWENTY-THREE

I WAS SURROUNDED BY wyrfangs, staring down the long conference table at Superhuman Security headquarters. All of them insisted on coming this time, and I couldn't blame them. A lot rode on what they learned here today.

Drym and Kragen sat on either side of me, the remaining four looming behind like gargoyles. I tried to get them all to sit, but they refused. Roul stood directly at my back. I no longer feared him. I recognized that he was wounded. Hurt by the refusal of the woman he thought was his friend to join them when they escaped.

We'd never be fist bumping buddies, but I saw him as the grumpy older brother of the group.

Zeus, the Society representative, brought more people with him this time as well. The two shifters from before were present—Behemoth and Russia—but there were others we hadn't met.

We'd arrived first and Zeus told us to get comfortable in the conference room while the others arrived. He introduced them as they came in. "You've met Russia and Behemoth. This is the rest of my team: Wasp, Ghost, Bull, Slick, Titan, and River. I apologize for the crowd. I tried to get them to stay home, but they're naturally curious."

Most wore interested expressions. I guess he'd told them about the wyrfangs, but there was nothing like seeing them in person.

I was a little shocked too. River was a woman. I'm not sure why I thought these supernaturals would be cave dweller alpha misogynists, but I had. She was gorgeous, but clearly capable of holding her own. One look and I knew she was a badass. I instantly wanted to be her when I grew up.

She gave me a wink when she caught me staring and I damn near swooned.

She walked right over to our end of the table and sat down next to Kragen. "Wow, you guys really are impressive." She leaned around him and stuck her hand out to me. "River. I'm a black bear shifter and I try to keep these guys civil, but it's not easy."

I reached to shake her hand and heard one of the others mumble.

"Did he just say you like popping eyeballs?"

She shrugged. "Never said I liked it, and Wasp isn't one to talk since he's a serious firebug with an explosions fetish."

"What?" My eyes darted around the room, trying to remember which one was Wasp.

Kragen interrupted my musings when he leaned forward. "It's good both full teams are here." He tapped a claw against the table and winced at the small divot he left behind. "We find we need more assistance than originally anticipated. They kept us largely ignorant of the outside world during our captivity, and we are struggling to navigate it. We'd also like to know more about Society to help us integrate, if possible."

One of the new men sat in the middle of the table and pulled out a laptop. Almost as tall as a wyrfang, he was lean, but clearly strong. A tattoo of thick swirling lines snaked up his arm and disappeared beneath the hem of his shirt sleeve.

His eyes seemed haunted, his movements slow and graceful. All except for his fingers, which were flying over the keys of the laptop.

"Zeus tasked me with finding BioSynth. They're good at hiding their tracks," he looked up with a grin, "but I'm better. I'll find them."

"In the meantime…" Zeus turned to the door and waved yet another person into the room. "I'd like to introduce you to Amelie Dumont."

A tiny woman walked in, followed by a chicken almost half her size. Her jaw dropped and she came to an abrupt halt.

The chicken ran into her legs, hopped back, and squawked "Fuck!" loud enough for everyone in the room to wince.

Amelie spun around and shook her finger at the bird. "I've told you not to follow so close. Serves you right." As she turned back to face the room, the chicken snaked its head back and forth and snapped its beak, clearly imitating her. "I saw that. Behave or I'm plucking out all your feathers."

Snickers erupted around the room when the chicken gasped.

Amelie directed a serene smile at us, clearly done arguing with poultry. "Please, call me Bacon. Everyone else does. My irritating companion is Meanosaurus."

"Your ancestors were paupers, while I am descended from great beasts!"

"You are a long way from the dinosaurs, Meanosaurus."

The chicken snorted but fell silent.

I surveyed the beasts around me and they all had identical confused expressions. I imagine the scene that just played out made as much sense to them as it did to me. Unless they had talking chickens in the lab. I was about to ask when Zeus took my attention.

"I asked Amelie to come because she's closely related to a council historian, and well suited to answer your questions about Society."

"Hold on to your butts." She threw her long, straight hair over her shoulder and tugged on a strap which brought a cross body bag around her hip. Her entire arm, up to the shoulder, disappeared inside the bag. It wasn't deep enough to hold her entire arm, but I'd just seen a chicken talk, so at this point I figured anything was possible.

Her arm reemerged with a stack of six binders in various colors balanced perfectly on her palm. She set the edge of the lowest one on the table and pushed them. They separated, spun in circles, and then slid down the table to rest in a neat line in front of us.

Drym leaned into my ear and whispered, "Why does she want us to hold our butts?"

"She's quoting a movie. It just means to get prepared."

His cold nose trailed up my neck, and I shivered.

"Well, that's not fair." River crossed her arms and leaned back in her chair. "I've been looking for my mate for years and these guys haven't been out of the lab for what? A month? And one of them's already found theirs."

She winked at me to let me know she was teasing, but I saw the envy in her eyes.

Bacon cleared her throat and sat on the tabletop, crossing her legs and leaning on one hand. "What you have in front of you is a primer of sorts. Most of Society history is verbal—handed down through the generations via stories. For obvious reasons, our predecessors didn't like leaving a paper trail. I've been slowly compiling a database of sorts, and I've hit the highlights for you. Each of the six binders covers a different species group. I expect you'll have questions once you've read them. My email is listed in the front of each one.

"As for navigating the normal world, that's best learned through observation and time. Since you clearly won't be walking around the town square at noon, it'll take longer, but you'll get there. Google is your friend. The internet isn't just for porn."

Her dark hair swung forward as she hopped off the table. She gave the man still typing furiously at his laptop a nod. "Bull."

He replied, "Bacon," without sparing her a glance.

"Right, I'm out. Zeus, thanks for the invite. It was worth the drive to get to see them." She turned toward us and grinned. "I can't wait for the council to get a load of you."

Then she and her chicken disappeared through the door.

TWENTY-FOUR

MY HEAD WAS SPINNING. They sheltered us from so much while in captivity, and the influx of people and talking chickens was too much to take in. I knew my brothers were also struggling. They'd moved in closer, crowding me, Kendal and Kragen where we sat at the table.

As kids, we piled together for comfort, and as adults, the instinct was still there. Huddle up, protect our pack.

Kendal sensed it. I noticed her muscles tense and her shoulders raise. "Um, Zeus?"

"Yes, Kendal?"

It bothered me he addressed her so informally, but I learned that most normals didn't require the formality that our captors did.

"I think this is a little overwhelming. Maybe we should adjourn, let the boys read over what Bacon brought, and then get together again later?"

"Of course. I apologize. This situation is so novel, I find myself a little out of my depth. I'll try to be more mindful in the future."

"They're overwhelmed?"

The one Zeus called Ghost mumbled from behind Behemoth, who I recognized from our first meeting. Behemoth's elbow shot back, causing Ghost to bend and grunt.

"Dude, I just meant they look cool as cucumbers. I wish I had a fraction of their control."

"Shut up, Ghost."

I nodded my thanks to the bear shifter, who nodded back.

Kragen stood, and Kendal and I followed suit. "Thank you for your assistance. We are grateful."

I gathered the binders and we turned to leave, but Kragen was still.

"You said at our last meeting that the council may provide a refuge for us?" His voice trailed off, leaving the question in the air.

"Yes. It's my understanding they are still deciding how to proceed, but I want you to know that no matter what you decide, Supe Sec will take care of you."

"Bull?"

The man at the laptop paused typing and looked up at Zeus, who tilted his head in our direction. "Oh, right. Yeah, we have tagged a few nearby properties that will work for a wyrfang compound. We're just waiting on the council to declare their intentions, and of course, you'll want to look before we put an offer on anything. All three are at least one hundred acres and most have a house already on site."

Kendal grabbed my forearm and I almost dropped the binders.

"Did you say one hundred acres?"

"Yes, ma'am."

"And you're going to buy it for them?"

Zeus chuckled. "Kendal, Society takes care of our own. Don't worry about the cost. Actually, I had Bull set up bank accounts for each of you. I deposited a bit of seed money, but the council will likely add a significant amount."

Bull slid a stack of envelopes from his bag and laid them on top of the binders. "Identities, bank cards, and cellphones, plus all the paperwork that goes with all of it. All the usual stuff. Each identity is new, but has a digital trail so you shouldn't have any trouble. Most people do everything online these days anyway, so it won't be suspicious that you aren't seen in person anywhere.

"I picked fairly common names, so I hope you don't hate them."

"I'm sure they'll be fine."

"Once you choose what name goes with what wyrfang, you shouldn't swap. Pick a name and stick with it."

"I understand."

I'm glad Kragen did. The only thing keeping me from shredding the table in frustration was Kendal pressed to my side. Roul's hands were clenched in tight fists, Cavi had shrunk in on himself and the others weren't faring much better.

We left the room in a single file, with Kendal pausing at the door. "How long will you and your brothers need to go over the binders?"

"Four days."

She seemed shocked at my answer, but didn't question it. She addressed Zeus from the doorway. "Meet again in five days? Same time?"

"That's fine." He looked around at his team. "I'll make sure most of them stay home."

She smiled, and a zing of jealousy stabbed my belly.

"Thank you." She nodded and then tilted her head to look up at me.

Her smile widened, and her eyes sparkled, erasing the jealousy completely.

"Let's go home."

I kept my hand on her lower back as we made our way from the building. When we arrived back at the cave, I set the binders and envelopes on the table and then swept her into my arms.

She squealed and swatted my chest playfully. I buried my nose deep into her hair and took several long, deep breaths. The world righted itself and I could think again.

My brothers were already digging into the envelopes by the time I could set Kendal on her feet.

Kragen distributed them randomly. "If you're seriously opposed to the name you got, we can trade."

Roul was the first to open his. "Butch Fisher. I like it."

Kendal giggled. "Butch suits you."

My brother grunted, but I saw him stand a little taller. One by one, the others opened their envelopes and read their official names. The shifter chose well, and everyone was happy with the aliases. Not that we would use them outside the normal world.

The identifications provided included a picture. I wasn't sure where Bull found the people depicted, but he chose well. They appeared to be strong, military type men. It would have been awkward if one of us was supposed to look like some of the scrawny scientists at the lab. I didn't think any of us could pull off meek or mild-mannered.

We turned our attention to Bacon's binders and Thurl rubbed at his neck.

"Kendal, would you mind reading in my place?"

"Of course not." She held out her hand and he gently set the binder on her palm.

I saw the relief course through him.

"Thank you."

She didn't ask why he didn't want to read, or tease him. She just gave him a smile and opened the book.

He stepped back, giving her a look of adoration, and my heart swelled for her. She didn't know he'd lost sight in one eye years ago. She didn't know how self-conscious he was.

She just stepped in to help.

It took everything I had to not grab her and swing her around in joy. My mate was perfect. She was kind, and brave, and everything I never knew I needed.

I swallowed a lump in my throat and opened my binder. Kragen had given me the information on shifters, and in the neatly typed table of contents I found "The Fates & Fated Mates."

My heart raced. As much as I wanted, I couldn't flip directly to that information. We'd agreed to brief each other on the topics in our binders, so none of us would need to read the entirety unless we wanted.

Kragen and I would read everything, but the others would pick the subjects they were interested in from each.

I wanted to make sure Kendal had a choice. That she could leave with no adverse effects. It was the last thing I wanted to happen, but it was important.

She shouldn't be tied unwillingly to a monster like me.

TWENTY-FIVE

I YAWNED SO HARD my jaw popped. Several heads rose around the table, their heads cocked and their ears pricked forward.

"Sorry guys, I'm a little tired."

I hadn't finished the sentence before Drym had me in his arms, striding away from the main space toward his room.

I still wasn't used to that. His quick action to get me whatever I needed. I'd say he could read my mind, but I knew he couldn't. I'd asked. I didn't want to leave while the others still worked on getting through their binders, but I knew arguing was futile. If I tried, the others would back Drym up in shooing me off to bed. I'd learned to just go with it.

It was amazing, really, how little sleep they needed. Being able to stay alert for so long made them better soldiers, but from my perspective, hearing their low voices echo through the cavern was soothing. A lullaby of safety and comfort.

Drym snuggled against my back, his warmth making me even more drowsy.

"Why does Thurl not like to read?"

He rubbed the underside of his jaw on the top of my head. "He lost the use of one eye completely, and the other strains when he tries to read. It was kind of you to take the task from him without question."

"Did he lose his eye the same way that Roul got his scars?"

I felt his chest rumble through my back as he chuckled. "No. Thurl lost sight in one eye while on a mission. They gave us faulty gear to see how we handled failure, and the premature explosion of a flash grenade sent shrapnel into his eye. Roul's ear notches and scars were won in a different battle. You should ask him to tell you about Texas."

I think I made a noise of assent, but I was already half asleep.

I dreamed I was running.

Not from rich assholes with nothing better to do with their time and money than stage human hunts, but from skinny nerds in lab coats. I woke up alone, drenched in cold sweat, and disoriented.

The cave system was always full of small sounds. Dripping water from somewhere deep underground and the hushed voices of the wyrfangs echoing down the tunnels were usually soothing, but I couldn't shake the note of fear my dream caused.

I stumbled to my feet and grabbed the small lantern Drym left for me. I couldn't navigate the entire system by myself, but I'd learned the path from Drym's room to the main chamber.

The six of them were crammed together, staring at an open binder. My toe caught a loose pebble and I found myself with six pairs of glowing eyes fixed on me.

It was unnerving.

Even though I knew them, and they were gentle and kind to me, I'd also seen firsthand how destructive and deadly they were. A shiver ran down my spine and I reassessed my thought that Bill pissing himself was totally overreacting.

The end of Roul's tail dragged back and forth on the ground, the *shush* of its sweep somehow ominous.

"What's wrong?" My voice wasn't as steady as I wanted.

Drym shook, his entire body shaking like a dog ridding itself of water. "We think…"

He looked around at his five brothers, and the pause stretched until I felt like I would snap.

"Just spit it out!"

All of them startled at my shout. Cavi even took a step back. Quin pushed his way in front of the others.

"We think your hunters are connected with our lab. Or at least one of them. And it's unclear if Society's counsel was as ignorant of their activities as they claim."

Roul punched him in the shoulder, which caused him to stumble several steps to the side.

"What's that for?"

"You are so blunt. Drym would have said it in an easier way."

Quin grumbled and rubbed at his smarting bicep. "Says the one who doesn't know what easy means."

"Knock it off, both of you."

I heard Drym admonish them, but my eyes were unfocused, my head full of fog. His warm, rough palms slid up and down the outside of my arms.

"Kendal, are you okay?"

I shook my head. "I just had a dream—nightmare. I was running from men in white coats." I looked up into his eyes, craning my neck back. "Lab coats."

He growled and crushed me to his chest. "They will not touch you."

I pushed out of his arms and stared up at him in horror. "It's not me I'm worried about. What if they get you?" I stepped to the side so I could see the others. "What if they get all of you?"

Roul's fists were clenching, Cavi had backed almost entirely out of the chamber, and the others were preternaturally still. After a few heartbeats, Kragen announced, "They won't. We will not go back. No matter what it takes."

That's exactly what I was afraid of. We needed to find these assholes, connected or not, and stop them permanently. I looked at Drym and nodded. "Okay then, we need to speed up our timeline. It's time for these pricks to sleep with the fishes."

Six heads cocked in confusion and I waved my hand. "It means it's past time for them to die."

Quin whooped. "I wasn't too keen on getting fish to make them beds, but that I can get behind."

I chuckled. "We need to contact Supe Sec. Hopefully they've found something."

"It's been barely a full day, Kendal. Our follow up meeting with them isn't until the end of the week." Drym stepped in close to me and some of the tension left my body.

"I know, but we have new information that might help them." I took a deep breath. "And they need to know their council may not be as innocent as they believe."

A few minutes later, I blinked against the bright sun at the cave entrance. I was blind until my eyes adjusted, and even then I would've killed for a pair of sunglasses. I pulled my cell phone out of my back pocket and checked the signal. Two bars.

"We need to get closer to civilization. I don't want the call to drop before I tell them everything that's happened."

Drym nodded and started walking, his palm on my lower back as always. I didn't mind.

"Did you finish your binder? The one about shifters?"

"Not entirely."

"But you've learned about fated mates?"

"Yes."

Nothing changed in his pace or demeanor. He still seemed calm and loose, but one-word answers weren't like him.

"What is it? What are you nervous about telling me?"

It took eight strides for him to tell me. I counted to keep myself from yelling.

"You should know that you hold the power in this, as in all things with me."

HELD BY A MONSTER

I nodded, but he wasn't looking at me. He stared straight ahead and kept a steady pace.

"Fated mates are much like you said. For shifters, there is one person who is your soul mate.

"Many years ago, the three fates became annoyed with Fenrir—essentially the father of shifters—and withheld mates. Just recently have they begun to find each other again."

A million questions ran through my mind, but somehow I managed to stay silent.

"The mate bond is unbreakable once in place."

He stopped and crouched in front of me, putting him at eye level.

"Do you understand, Kendal? If you choose to accept me as mate, and we forge the bond, it can never be undone."

KENZIE KELLY

TWENTY-SIX

MY EYES BORED INTO hers as we stood frozen in the forest. I don't think I drew breath until she nodded.

"I understand."

"It is your decision to make, and I urge you to think well before you make it. To consider everything before you decide."

She nodded and we walked in silence for a while.

"Do you not want me as your mate?"

Her voice was small and hesitant and I hated it. I whirled and wrapped my frame around hers. I had to bend and fold. She was so small, seemed so fragile, but I'd seen her strength.

"I want nothing more."

I heard her swallow. "I sense a *but* there."

I sucked air through my muzzle and licked the side of her neck. I scraped my teeth gently against her flesh and felt her shiver in my arms. "But I am a monster, and I fail to see how you could be happy tied to me forever."

She pushed at my chest and I let her go.

"My first instinct is to rail at you and tell you that you can't decide that for me, but you said that already, so I'll rein it in. I think the future is too uncertain for either of us to make big decisions right now." She looked away and sighed. "Let's deal with the problems in front of us, then decide how we can be together and both of us be happy."

My brain caught on the 'we' part of her statement. I wanted to whoop for joy, but it was premature. She wasn't choosing me... yet. But she was giving me a chance. Maybe she could learn to live with a monster. Maybe even come to care for one.

She checked her phone and said, "This is far enough."

She pulled up the shifter's contact and I heard the line ring.

"Kendal, is everything all right?" Zeus's voice was clear.

I thought she'd reach a receptionist or secretary. Why did she have his direct line?

"No, not really. We've found some new information and it's important to share."

"Understood. Will you come tonight?"

She looked up at me, but I didn't understand the question in her eyes.

"Actually, I think you should come to us this time."

I nodded in agreement. It was a risk, allowing them to see where we hid, but it was also an advantage to be on our turf for this discussion. I think the shifters were trustworthy, but seeing them in our space might help solidify those feelings.

And if they betrayed us, it would be easier to conceal the bodies.

Kendal gave him our location and chuckled. I'd lost the thread of conversation, so I didn't know what she thought was funny.

"I think that's best. Although if you also wanted to bring Bacon, it wouldn't be amiss. I know the guys have questions for her."

"Already?"

"Yes. Turns out they don't sleep much. They'll wait for you just inside the tree line and show you the way."

"Good. Until tonight then."

The call ended and she looked at me. "They'll be here at nightfall. What should we do until then?"

"Um…" I didn't know what sort of activities she would like, or what we could do given my appearance hampering our options.

"If I ran, would you chase me?"

Instantly, my dick filled and pressed at the back of my seam. I shoved my palm against it, trying in vain to keep it hidden.

"You like that idea."

"I like that idea very much," I confirmed, "but I am afraid it will trigger you."

"Or, it might help me free some trauma to know that instead of dogs and guns, it's my monstrous guardian chasing me."

The dappled sunlight through the trees made her eyes sparkle. My tongue was tied in knots at the thought of chasing Kendal through the woods.

In a flash, she grinned and took off. A wild bolt through the trees that seemed random, but she kept to the general direction back to our cave. I counted to twenty to give her a head start.

My muscles bunched and strained against the urge to run until finally I let loose. I dropped to all fours and the ground rushed under my belly. She looked over her shoulder and squealed when she saw me, but it was too late. I'd caught her.

I pounced and rolled. I kept her well protected in my arms and came to rest on my back, holding her on top of me while she laughed.

"That's not fair," she pouted. "I forgot you were so fast."

I rolled her beneath me and pressed my length into the warm heat at the juncture of her thighs.

She gasped and her eyes closed as she pressed up into me.

"When it comes to catching you, I will never be fair."

She grabbed the waistband of her pants and pushed while I stared in shock.

"I can get us to the cave."

Her head rolled from one side to the other. "I don't care if the squirrels watch, and there's no one else out here. You'd have heard if there was, right?"

My mouth went dry and I swallowed hard. "Yes. I would hear them."

She managed to get her pants and panties off and pressed herself against me. "You caught me. Now I want a prize."

I groaned and slid my cock against her wet folds. I buried my nose in her hair and my back arched as I felt how wet she was. "I'm not sure I can control myself. I don't want to hurt you."

"I don't want you to control yourself, and you won't hurt me."

I looked for any hesitation in her eyes and found none. "What do you want?"

"I want my monster to fuck me in the woods."

TWENTY-SEVEN

YOU KNOW THE PHRASE, be careful what you ask for? In this case it was bullshit. I got exactly what I asked for, and every second was glorious.

As soon as the words left my mouth it was like a tether snapped on Drym's control. He shoved inside me with one rough jerk on my shoulders. As he withdrew, I felt the spikes along his shaft scrape against me in the most delicious way.

My eyes rolled back in my head and my orgasm hit with an intensity that had my entire body shaking. My limbs went limp, but almost immediately I was spinning up again as he pounded into me with powerful strokes.

Every time he bottomed out, his knot hit my clit and sent a fresh wave of ecstasy through my veins. I moaned as a second orgasm hit with even greater force. My blood rushed through my ears and every nerve in my body was on fire and it was too much and not enough all at once.

His forearms wrapped beneath me, cushioning me from the hard ground. One hand wrapped around my shoulder and the other gripping the globe of my ass. I felt the tiny pinpricks of his claws as they bit into my flesh and the pain spiked another round of pleasure.

His rhythm became jerky and his pauses while buried deep inside of me longer and I knew he was close.

His long, forked tongue swept across my lips, and I opened for him. His tongue swept into my mouth, curling around mine and sliding backwards in the wyrfang's version of a kiss.

I felt his tail curling around my calf and sliding up my leg. I gasped when it wrapped around where we were joined and then again when I felt it press into my small hole. The tip pushed inside and I felt so full my mind shattered. His tongue was down my throat, his tail in my ass, and his cock plundered my pussy. He owned me, body and soul.

My third orgasm left me wrecked. Wrung out and boneless. I couldn't even hold my arms around him as he filled me completely. He howled when he came, the sound one of triumph and joy.

He kept us joined when he rolled onto his back.

I couldn't move. I was aware we were both panting to catch our breath, that his cum leaked from me and coated our bellies, but beyond the bubble of our bodies nothing existed.

I think I fell asleep. The sun was high in the sky when he chased me, and now it was low enough to dim the forest to a magical gloom.

"Sunset approaches."

I made an incoherent noise.

He shifted me like a baby, carrying me against his chest as he made his way to a lake. He carried me straight into the water, his body heat keeping the worst of the chill at bay. He cleaned us with his hands without ever putting me down.

He supported my weight as he dressed me, then carried me to the cave. I only perked up when I realized he intended to take me to his room.

"The meeting is in the main cavern." I sounded sleepy, but I wasn't.

"You need to rest."

"What I need," I said as I grabbed his muzzle to force him to look at me, "is to be at that meeting."

His eyes closed, the twin golden glow winking out. It was several breaths before they reopened and he turned toward the large room. Without thinking, I patted his chest and said, "Good boy."

He snorted. "If you expect my tail to wag and thump against the floor, you'll be disappointed."

I giggled.

We rounded a bend and stepped into the chamber. Eight sets of eyes turned to stare this time. Zeus and Bull quickly returned their gaze to the laptop, but Bacon—who sat cross-legged on the table—whistled.

She looked at the wyrfangs—actually; she looked at their crotches. "I don't know where they're hiding them, but they must know how to use them."

She hopped off the table and came around, holding her palm over her head.

I laughed and pushed against Drym until he set me down. "Is it that obvious?"

"Maybe not to everybody, but the energy rolling off you two is sexy times on steroids."

I high-fived the diminutive witch and we both dissolved into laughter.

"I don't know what y'all are going on about, but there's no bugs in this cave. I was promised cave bugs." Meanosaurus squawked her displeasure at the lack of insects and strutted under the table.

Bacon and I fell into another fit of giggles.

I think I was sex drunk. Was that a thing? Could you get drunk from multiple, earth-shattering, muscle melting orgasms?

It had to be a thing.

Mate bond or not, I was ruined for anyone but Drym.

We'd hash out the details later, but there was no way I was leaving him. Being together would be hard, but not as hard as tracking two sets of bad guys and fighting against a possibly corrupt system.

When Bacon and I sobered I turned to the wyrfangs spread around the table. "What have you told them so far?"

Kragen answered. "Nothing. They've just arrived."

I nodded and waited for someone to speak. Anyone. For several long minutes we all just stared at each other. I wasn't sure what was happening, but it was awkward as hell. All the 'fangs were bowed up and tense, almost posturing.

Bacon broke the tension. "If y'all need to whip 'em out and measure, get on with it. Otherwise, there are things we should talk about instead of staring at each other wondering whose dick is bigger."

I laughed and caught Kragen and Zeus both smiling.

"It is difficult for us to accept others in our space. I apologize," Kragen addressed Bacon.

She just waved. "Noted. Get on with it."

"Kendal said you had new information to share that couldn't wait." Zeus tilted his head toward Bull and his laptop. "We've found a few things as well."

Kragen nodded. "It's possible the director of BioSynth is one of Kendal's hunters. After going through the binders Bacon provided, we've caught mentions of a Mr. Blue associated with your council. Mr. Blue is one of the primaries in the group who abducted and hunted Kendal. It seems too coincidental for there to be two Mr. Blues operating in the area."

Zeus was shaking his head. "If that's true, then at least one council member surely knows what he was up to. I don't want to believe any of them would condone such a thing, but Society isn't above cruelty any more than normals."

Bacon was rummaging through her large pack, her hand shoved inside to the shoulder. She eventually emerged with a small notebook, which she flipped through until landing on a page near the middle.

She looked up when she realized everyone had gone silent. "Right. So I might track the council members for various reasons, none of which I can talk about outside Jackal Division, so don't ask. A man, commonly referred to as Mr. Blue because he always has something blue in his outfit, has been linked with the fae council member."

"Why would the fae be interested in creating a were/dragon hybrid?"

Drym moved to my other side as he spoke, unconsciously closing ranks with his brothers.

Bacon, Zeus, and Bull all shared a look before Bacon answered. "Because the fae have always felt like they should be in charge."

TWENTY-EIGHT

"I DON'T UNDERSTAND." I felt like I spoke for all of us, given the confused looks on my brother's faces.

It was Zeus who explained. "A hierarchy of sorts exists in the council. Dragons have always held the tie-breaking vote on any matter and act as the ultimate peacekeepers. The longest lived among us, their experience borne of longevity is seen as the best for ruling over the entirety of Society. They often defer to the wider council on small matters, but in the end, their word is law.

"And the fae don't appreciate it. They have always felt like they should be in charge—or at least hold equal power."

Bacon continued, "So imagine you wanted to stage a coup against the most powerful supernaturals. You are no match for them, so you need something that is."

"So you create a creature that is a blend of weres and dragons." My mind whirled, stunned at the implication that we were created for a political takeover.

"Exactly," Zeus said.

"Why weres? Why not a more powerful supernatural?" I quickly added, "No offense."

Zeus chuckled. "None taken. Bull, you want to weigh in on this?"

The shifter paused his typing to look up. "I suspect they wanted our healing ability. Dragons are tough, but if you pierce their scales, they are vulnerable. We can rapidly heal from just about any injury. Dragons heal at the same rate as humans. Plus, the fae are smart enough not to give humans a weapon so powerful it could overthrow all of us, but egotistical enough to think they could retain control over any creature created. They needed something to threaten the dragons, and appease the human's need for weapons, but not something that could take over Society as a whole."

Kragen was shaking his head. "I still don't understand how we would be a viable weapon against dragons. From the information Bacon provided, their scales are almost impenetrable."

Bacon was nodding as she crawled back on top of the table to sit cross-legged. She reached out and grabbed my wrist, pulling it and me forward until I was against the table.

HELD BY A MONSTER

She held my hand up and pointed to my claws. "I think your answer lies here." She pressed the tip of her finger to the tip of my claw, and blood welled from the puncture. "These don't look like shifter or dragon claws. They are too curved and sharp-edged." She took my index finger and dragged it lightly over the surface of the table, where it left a deep groove. "Were claws are softer—able to cut through flesh but breakable. Dragon claws are a bit stronger, but not enough to penetrate a dragon's hide. Yours are like hardened steel. I suspect they can cut through dragon scales like butter."

"She has a point." Cavi stepped closer from his usual place against the wall. "Our claws only break under extreme duress and they are sharp enough to damage every tested surface."

I winced as I remembered the lengths the scientists went to get readings on how much every part of us could withstand.

Cavi reached up, brushing the tip of his broken horn and I knew he also remembered.

"Surely a team of six couldn't wipe out an entire species?" I carefully took my hand back from Bacon, and she smiled up at me.

Zeus sighed. "No. Even before we knew about the council connection, we believed there were plans to create many more wyrfangs when their experiments yielded the results they wanted. The human military wouldn't want just one squad if they could have multiple."

"Well, shit."

That from Quin, who had remarkably remained quiet.

Kendal leaned into my side. "So it's important we stop these bastards. We need to work faster."

Bull looked over at Bacon. "I don't suppose there's an artifact that could—."

"No. Nope. Not happening." She slashed her hand through the air. "No way, no how."

Bull sighed. "Fine." He turned back to his laptop screen. "I think I have a way to discover Mr. Blue's real identity, but I don't think anyone's going to like it."

I took a deep breath and looked at my brothers. Roul was glowering more than usual, Cavi had retreated to the side of the cave, and Quin was practically bouncing in excitement. Thurl crossed his arms and stood barely moving. Kragen and I shared a resigned look.

As long as the plan didn't involve Kendal, or provide an opportunity for her to be hurt, we could work with it.

Kragen nodded. "Let's hear it."

"We need to draw them both out—the fae and Mr. Blue." He looked up at us. "We need to offer them something they can't refuse."

I heard Kendal suck in a breath next to me. "No. That's not happening. We can draw out Mr. Blue using me as bait and figure out how to get the fae later."

I growled and snapped my teeth, my tail swinging in agitation. "Absolutely not."

She whirled and poked me in the chest. "Do you know what he's suggesting?" Her voice was low and furious. "He's suggesting we use one of you as bait."

I nodded. "That's preferable."

"For who?" She turned and looked at everyone else in the chamber. "They have spent their entire lives in captivity. We are not putting them at risk of ending up right back there."

"We can mitigate the risk. We'll take every precaution—"

"It won't be enough!" She screamed and slapped her hand on the table. "These men hunted me. They abducted me in broad daylight in a public parking lot! They will stop at nothing to get what they want. Do you think this fae council member is going to get squeamish about mowing through your entire team?"

She pointed at Zeus. "Because I don't think they will. They will do everything in their power to get the 'fangs back under their control. They know that recapturing one means getting them all, because no way in hell they'll ever leave a brother behind."

She faced me again. "Tell me I'm wrong."

I shook my head, my ears flat against my head. "You aren't wrong." I reached for her but she jerked away.

TWENTY-NINE

"THIS IS BULLSHIT!" I was screaming like a seagull and I didn't care. Tears tracked down my face and I angrily brushed them away.

Drym reached for me again and this time I let him pull me into his arms. The underside of his jaw pressed into the back of my head and his warmth seeped through me. My anger gave way to despair.

I loved him.

The realization hit me like I was being tagged in dodgeball. I'd fallen in love with him and the very idea that they could recapture or kill him made my heart shrivel into a tiny marble.

I felt more than heard his words, my ear pressed tightly to his chest. "It will be alright. We will plan for every contingency." He chuckled without mirth. "It's what they designed us for, after all."

"I'll go."

Everyone's heads swung to Roul. He stood staring at the ground, his posture stiff, his hands curled into fists.

Kragen was shaking his head. "You know you can't. We will need you in case something goes wrong." He looked at Zeus. "The same goes for Thurl, Cavi, and Quin. It has to be me or Drym."

I knew, before the decision was made, that it would be Drym. Kragen was first in command, the most strategic mind. Drym was no slouch, but even he'd admitted Kragen was first and he was second for good reason.

I wrapped my arms around Drym's waist and held on tight. It was irrational, but my mind was telling me that if I somehow managed to hang on, nothing bad could happen to him. I could keep him from going.

Eventually he lifted me into his arms, cuddling me close as I cried. I didn't listen to the others making their plans. Drym crouched with me still curled in his arms and I cried myself to sleep.

I woke up when he stood. The others wore grim faces, even Bacon.

Bull was packing away his laptop, signaling the meeting was over.

"Can we put a tracker on him?"

The others seemed startled I was awake.

"Just in case?"

Cavi was shaking his head. "They will scan him from head to toe. They'll be expecting it."

Zeus looked directly at me. "With the mate bond in place, you might be able to track him. The bond works differently for weres and dragons. Weres typically can feel their mate's emotions, even across vast distances. The dragon bond is more like a tether, from what I understand. Invisible to everyone but the mated pair, it's like a string that connects them so they can find their way to one another across the globe."

I felt Drym stiffen beneath me. Did he not know that? Did he not want that? I crawled from his arms and looked at him, ready to tell him to forge the bond right then and there, but the look on his face stopped me.

As long as they didn't intend to take him away right that second, I had time. I would wait until we were alone and then find out why he seemed so resistant to the idea.

Sure, he'd said earlier he wanted me to think over the implications of being mated for life before making the decision, but time was the one thing we didn't have.

There were issues that needed to be sorted, but that would just have to happen later.

"So what's the plan?"

Zeus and Kragen shared a look and Zeus launched into how they planned to trap a madman and a fae. "I'll ask to meet with a fae acquaintance tomorrow at dusk. We often share information, so it isn't out of the ordinary for us to meet this way. While I'm speaking with him Drym will reveal himself as if on accident.

"That should be enough to get the attention of both the fae council member and Mr. Blue. All we have to do from there is wait for one—or preferably both—of them to show up."

"What if the fae doesn't tell the council member what they see during your meeting?" I tugged at my shirt hem, but it wasn't my clothes making me so uncomfortable.

Zeus chuckled. "Oh, he will. He's notorious for his inability to keep a secret."

I nodded because if I tried to speak I'd break down in tears again.

Bacon and Bull packed up their computers. She hopped off the table and scanned the room, even looking under the single piece of furniture and around the other 'fangs. She stood up and sighed.

"Cluck, cluck, Meanosaurus! Time to go!"

HELD BY A MONSTER

Several of the 'fangs winced at the volume of her voice.

Bull snorted. "How often do you lose that bird?"

Bacon mumbled something that sounded suspiciously like, "Not often enough."

With a squawk and wings that flapped furiously, the fowl in question emerged from a tunnel. Her beak was clamped around insects stacked three deep and two high. All I could really see of her face was wriggling legs and the end of her wide, stretched beak.

Quin reared back in horror. "That's disgusting."

Meanosaurus said something unintelligible.

Bacon rolled her eyes. "It's bad manners to talk with your mouth full."

The chicken *harrumphed*, which was another new experience for me.

Roul took the lead, showing them the way out of the cave system.

"It's three o'clock in the morning. I'll be back around three this afternoon for any final preparations." Zeus was the last to leave, giving me one last, weighted look before disappearing into the gloom.

I don't know if it was the stress, or the energy expended during all the mind blowing orgasms, but I was drained. I grabbed my small lantern and made my way back to Drym's room. My feet felt made of lead and my fingertips dragged the ground. Metal pellets replaced my brain and every sound was replaced with a dull *whoosh*.

I only knew Drym followed me from the heat of his hand on my lower back.

When we got to the room, I collapsed onto the pile of blankets. I didn't look up at him. My head was too heavy for my neck to lift.

"I want to forge the bond."

THIRTY

EVEN THOUGH I KNEW that's what she was going to say, it still made my skin tingle. Whether in anticipation or fear, I didn't know.

I shook my head. "I don't think that's a decision that should be made under these circumstances."

She snorted. "What circumstances would you prefer? When we're old and gray and the only thing left ahead of us is death? Are you afraid, or do you not want to bond with me?"

I strangled my whine. "I don't want you to feel pressured."

She lifted her head and stared at me with tired eyes. "It's too late for that."

I huffed and looked away. "No, it's not. You can take all the time you need to make an informed decision. There is no reason to be hasty."

She sprung from my bed and I backed up as she advanced on me.

"No reason to be hasty? Are you fucking kidding me?" Her little hands fisted at her sides. "Tomorrow night you're going to reveal yourself to someone who will run to tell their boss, who is one of the people that funded the research to create you! Someone who will tell the director of the lab!"

I shrugged. "That's the easy part."

"Easy?"

I winced as she screeched.

"If that's easy, what's hard?"

I took a deep breath and cocked my head. "The waiting that comes after."

Her entire body deflated and she sank to the blankets. "That's what I'm afraid of. I don't think I'll survive the wait without some kind of connection to you."

"I'll be fine."

"You can't say that. You don't know what's going to happen."

I growled low in my throat. "I will always come back to you. I don't need a forged mate bond to tell me what lengths I'd go to in order to get back to your side. I would endure a thousand lifetimes of captivity if it meant you were safe."

"Don't you see?" Tears tracked down her cheeks. "If I don't have a way to feel that you're okay, I'll be in hell."

I crouched in front of her and licked her cheek. She turned away from me, and I wanted to shatter into a million pieces. "I can't feel like I've pressured you into a lifetime tethered to a monster."

"I don't see you as a monster. You've protected me—cared for me—since the moment I crashed into your legs. You've made me feel safe. You've never belittled me or made me feel stupid." Her chest rose with a big inhale. "I didn't fall in love with a monster. I fell in love with you."

My ears flicked back and forth, filled with the sound of blood rushing through my veins. My mind was blank, my muscles locked in place. On a whisper, I asked, "Did you say you love me?"

"Yes, Drym. I love you."

My mouth watered. "You want to forge a mate bond with me?" I waved my hands at my body, not fully comprehending how this could happen. How did I get so lucky, not only to have found my fated mate, but to have her say she loved me?

How was a creature grown in a lab, designed for dealing death, worthy of love?

I stalked toward her on all fours. She waited until my nose was so close to her face, I felt her breath.

"Yes. I want to forge a mate bond with you."

Unwilling to wait another second, I ripped at her pants.

She laughed. "Oh, it's forged with sex? Bonus!"

She helped me undress her. When she was fully naked I sat back on my paws, wanting to etch every line of her body into my memory. "You are gorgeous."

I didn't wait for her to answer. I could smell her arousal, could see how wet she was for me when she spread her legs. I bent over her, tilting my muzzle toward her shoulder. As I shoved my cock into her delicious heat, I bit down hard and fast.

Euphoria filled me. She orgasmed and her cunt squeezed me like a vise as I withdrew. She moaned as I thrust again. The taste of her blood, like the sweetest wine, coated my tongue.

"Holy shit, you bit me."

My fangs were still buried in the soft swell between her shoulder and neck and I was reluctant to let go. Bacon's information didn't say how long the bite should last for the bond to be complete, only that I had to bite her.

As Kendal had said, the sex was a bonus.

HELD BY A MONSTER

Her arms and legs wrapped around me and she urged me on as I pounded her into the blankets. I felt possessed. Thank everything holy that she made keening sounds of pleasure because I couldn't stop.

Another orgasm ripped through her and I closed my eyes to savor the feel of her walls clenched around me, the way my spikes bent back and forth as I moved. My rear claws scrabbled at the rock as I tried to force myself deeper, but I was already at the limit of her body.

I gasped and let go when an odd sensation popped in my ears. My fur stood on end and it felt like static electricity filled the air. A strange golden glow cocooned us.

"Are you seeing this?" She panted and her hips still moved against mine, but her eyes were open in wonder.

"Yes, I see it."

There was nothing in Bacon's notes about this. The light pulsed with us as I took her. It grew brighter and brighter until we both had to shut our eyes against it. I couldn't hold back any longer when I felt her third release. I spent myself inside her, the light behind my eyelids impossibly bright before it winked out.

I rolled onto my back and situated her against my chest. We both stared in awe at the tiny golden motes of light that danced around us.

She reached a hand for one, and it moved away, like there was a bubble between it and her. "They're so beautiful."

"Do you think they're our tether?" I rumbled, quiet as if being loud would break the spell.

She giggled. "I don't know. Having dancing lights no one else can see isn't as weird as a talking chicken, so it's possible."

She rubbed her hand up my chest and around my neck. "You bit me."

I nodded. "It was the bite that forged the bond."

"So, the sex was…?"

I grinned. "A bonus."

THIRTY-ONE

THE TINY DANCING GOLD lights were still there when I woke up. Only now, they stretched out the door of the room.

I rummaged around in my suitcase and found a clean pair of jeans and a t-shirt. I had no idea what time it was, but it was before dusk. Drym wouldn't leave without saying goodbye.

I didn't bother with the lantern. The swaying lights led the way. I could hear voices in the main cavern, but no one was shouting or seemed upset.

I regretted not bothering with shoes when I stubbed my big toe on a loose rock. I hadn't even finished my curse when Drym came running around the corner.

He lifted me into his arms and carried me back into the room, where Zeus and the rest of the 'fangs were bent over scattered papers on the table.

"Cavi, get the first aid kit. Kendal's hurt her toe."

"How did you know I hurt my toe?"

He smirked and poked himself in the forearm with the tip of a claw.

The same spot on my forearm pinched. "Ow!" It took a minute for me to catch on. "Oh…" I looked at Zeus. "But I thought weres felt emotions, not physical things."

He nodded. "I've never seen any were mates react to their mate being injured the way you two just did."

Cavi stepped up with the first aid kit. "Since we are a blend of two species of shifter, it's to be expected our bonds will behave differently from either of the contributor's."

"Which might explain that we see dancing lights instead of a more rope-like tether, right?"

Cavi's head tilted as he thought. "Yes, that's the most likely explanation."

"I can't believe you got both." Zeus was shaking his head. "I'm almost jealous, but I'm not sure I'd want to feel every paper cut my mate gets."

"Speaking of—" I gasped as Cavi poured antiseptic on my toe. "When do I get to meet your mates?"

He quickly threw his hands up. "Oh, I'm not mated. Only two of my team have been so lucky." He looked away and cleared his throat. "I'm not sure, but I promise we'll get the three of you together soon."

"I'll hold you to that promise. Especially if they take the bait."

"I understand." He gave me a sympathetic smile before turning his attention back to what I could now see was a map.

Kragen pointed to the parking lot behind my apartment building, and the tree line. "Zeus will meet with the fae here." He moved his claw an inch into the woods. "Drym will be here. After you engage the fae in conversation, he will move up to here"—his claw drew closer to the parking lot—"before walking parallel to the tree line for several yards."

"If my contact sees him, I'll use the word orange so Drym knows to break off. If I don't, then Drym will retrace his steps, passing by us again and continuing in that direction." He smirked. "Fae eyesight is better than humans. I don't think we'll need the return trip."

My heart threatened to beat out of my chest. I tried to take solace in the fact that they all seemed so calm, but it didn't work. I was the only one freaking out.

I wasn't built for this. I wasn't some superhuman security dude (pun intended), or a genetically engineered killing machine. I was just a human. A female human, who would have died that night in the woods if it weren't for Drym.

I didn't have any special skills. I couldn't survive for weeks with only a piece of string or something. I barely made it through Damruck summers with the air conditioning going full blast. I'd go to three different stores if my main one was out of my specific brand of toothpaste.

I was as far from badass as a person could get. Why did I think I could ever help them?

"Kendal, did you ever see the men in charge? Well enough to recognize them?" Kragen's body was loose, relaxed.

Mine threatened to snap into pieces it was wound so tight. I managed a nod. "The three key guys, I think, were the ones that came down soon after they put me in the basement cage. They looked over each of us and then gave us numbers. A fourth man took notes." I swallowed. "I would recognize those four, like I recognized Bill."

Kragen nodded, but Zeus's eyebrows slashed down.

"Who's Bill?"

Drym answered for me. "One of the men who tried to recapture Kendal."

Zeus nodded. "How many were there?"

"Three." My voice was surprisingly strong and it gave me a speck of confidence. I looked Zeus dead in the eyes. "No survivors."

He nodded. "We have cleanup crews when needed. I'll give you their contact information."

Drym's warm hand trailed up my back. I didn't need the comfort. I wasn't sad those men were dead. They were awful human beings. Maybe that made me a bad person, but at that point, I just didn't care.

"Since you're doing this in my apartment's parking lot, can I go to my apartment?"

Drym's growl at my back was low, but instead of raising the hairs on my neck like it probably should have, it made me lean into him.

The dancing lights of our bond pulsed brighter.

I was such a goner.

I knew I was going to fall for him. I resisted because what kind of future could we have? Now that we were bonded, I wondered why I was worried in the first place. We would make it work. We were meant to be together. The fates decreed it.

Everything would work out the way it was supposed to.

If I kept telling myself that, I might actually believe it.

Zeus nodded at Drym. "I can escort Kendal to her apartment before I get into position."

Drym's hand flexed on my back.

I turned and patted his chest. "Roul is watching over everything. I'll be fine locked in my apartment. It's you I'm worried about."

His chest rose and fell beneath my hand. His eyes closed and he snuffled into my hair. He straightened and a look passed between him and Kragen I couldn't interpret. Kragen nodded.

Why did I think they'd just made a deal I really wouldn't like?

THIRTY-TWO

I PROWLED THE WOODS, just out of sight of the tree line. My eyes flicked between Zeus, who leaned against a black SUV, and Kendal's window. She'd turned the lamp on for me. I hadn't thought to ask her, but being able to see her pass by every so often gave me a sense of peace.

Kragen's assurance that if something went wrong, they'd save Kendal first, didn't hurt.

My instincts screamed that something would go sideways. I felt the same way before the mission that took Thurl's sight. I couldn't put my finger on it, but something was off.

We had gone through every aspect of our plan several times. We made minor adjustments, but in the end neither I nor Kragen could find any fault with it.

So why was I so unsettled?

The thin line of glowing dots stretched between me and Kendal. I had to look to see them, and they faded out in my peripheral vision. I was fine as long as they didn't disappear entirely.

I had no idea that when Kendal asked to bond that it would be just as welcome for me. Knowing I could find her, that I would feel if she were injured, gave me reassurance I didn't think possible.

As long as she was okay, it didn't matter what happened to me.

Headlights swept the trees around me and my ears pricked. A low-slung sports car pulled up next to Zeus and a tall, lanky man got out.

His short blond hair was an artfully arranged tousle meant to look like he'd rolled out of bed that way, but it probably took hours to perfect. He walked with a rolling gait as he rounded the hood of his car and stuck his hand out for Zeus.

"Aymar."

"Zeus. Why have you brought me to the back of beyond?"

His voice was soft, but had a note of steel.

"Like I said, I have information to pass along."

The fae looked around and scrunched his face. "Well, pass it along. I don't want to stay here long."

HELD BY A MONSTER

Zeus shook his head. "Impatient, as always I see." Zeus's voice took on a hard edge. "I'll need something from you in exchange."

"Of course." Aymar waved his hand in an airy circle.

"I've come across some knowledge of a new creature existing right here in Damruck."

He tried to hide it, but I could see the fae's demeanor perk up. "What sort of new creature?"

"One capable of taking on dragons."

Aymar's hand fluttered around his neck, but his shock was only performance deep. "Well, that is a worthy piece of news."

"Word on the street is that these creatures are associated with a human."

That was my cue. I moved closer to where the two men stood. I kicked a pinecone, sending it skittering in front of me as I made my way through the sparse pines.

I kept my nose pointed deeper into the woods. My eyes would give too much of my location away.

I'd gone maybe fifteen feet when I heard Aymar gasp.

"Did you see that?"

"I saw a firefly flicker orange."

"No, not that."

I moved deeper into the woods, having confirmation I'd been seen. A low hum directed my attention skyward. The dim light of a small moon made it hard to see, but the object darting overhead had followed us on so many missions, it was easy to recognize.

"Drone!" I called out to my brothers stationed nearby. I didn't have time to do anything more. Multiple soft whistles heralded the hundreds of darts that rained down on me. I threw my forearms over my head and roared in frustration. There was nothing I could do.

"Stand down! Regroup. Kendal will know where to find me."

Men in tactical gear, weapons raised and eyes wide darted toward me. My vision went blurry. I sank on my haunches and held my palms out. If I could escape capture without serious injury it would better my chances during any rescue attempt.

I sought Kendal's window as nets wrapped around my body from three directions. Her hands were pressed against the glass, her face ashen. The fear in her eyes was the last thing I saw before the drugs sucked me under.

It wasn't the first time I'd been drugged, and I knew it would wear off quickly. I'd also learned to stay still and silent, feigning unconsciousness for as long as possible. The time to assess my situation was invaluable.

HELD BY A MONSTER

The scientists always put more faith in their sedatives than they should.

Slowly, the sounds separated and became distinct. I was inside a transport, my wrists and ankles bound. Two guards rode in the back with me, and I heard a driver and a scientist from the front.

The guards were whispering, trying to keep their conversation unnoticed.

"Can you believe this shit? What is that thing?"

"I don't know, but I hope like hell it doesn't wake up before we get to the facility. I don't want to tangle with it."

"Aww, c'mon Carl. It gave up without a fight. Maybe they have some sort of control over it."

"Or maybe it knew the drugs were gonna knock it out and decided to bide its time."

"I think we could take it. Nothing survives a point-blank rifle shot."

I'd love to tell him that he would need to make damn sure the bullet entered my brain. And hope my reflexes were so dulled I didn't gut him before he could pull the trigger.

I tuned them out and focused on the front of the vehicle. The scientist's voice seemed familiar, but I couldn't place it. She was quietly giving the driver directions, which the driver acknowledged with grunts. Neither of them were as chatty as my two guards.

It didn't matter. Like the smarter one said, I would bide my time. They would make a mistake. They always did.

THIRTY-THREE

I WAS HYPERVENTILATING. I knew it, Zeus knew it, the other 'fangs knew it. Cavi was desperately trying to get me to slow my breathing. Quin hovered behind him, his normally lackadaisical demeanor gone.

"Cavi, do something."

"What do you think I'm doing, Quin?"

"He's going to kill us."

Quin moved behind me and I felt a whisper as his hands came up.

"What are you doing?"

"Getting ready to catch her if she passes out. The least we can do is make sure she doesn't get a traumatic brain injury."

I wanted to laugh at that, but I couldn't get enough oxygen. My lungs were the size of marbles, and not the big ones either.

My vision was going black at the edges. At least Quin would keep me from hitting my head. I didn't want Drym to experience me getting a concussion.

Big, dark eyes appeared in my narrow field of vision. Why was Bacon in my apartment? Her icy hands framed my cheeks and sucked more of my precious little breath away. Her skin was like ice.

Her hands moved down the sides of my neck, coming to rest over my collarbones. A pulse of energy crackled down my spine and suddenly I could breathe again. My vision cleared and my lungs expanded.

I closed my eyes and just breathed until I assured myself my body was once again under my control.

"Thank you." I managed to croak at the smaller woman.

She waved her hands through the air. She tried to smile, but couldn't quite pull it off. She blew on her fingertips, singed red and angry looking. "Don't mention it."

"What happened?"

Quin handed me a bottle of water. "Panic attack."

"Not with me." I rolled my eyes. "I know I was having a panic attack. I meant to Bacon."

"Oh, well." She winced as Cavi spread cream on her hands. "I'm an energy witch, so I just gave your body a bit of a reset button."

"Did you burn your hands?"

She snorted. "Yeah, well, that's the thing. I can't use my abilities without getting shocked. The more I want to regulate the energy flowing out of me, the more damage is done."

I must have looked horrified because she immediately started trying to reassure me.

"It's okay, really! I don't use my abilities often and all things considered, electrical burns heal pretty fast."

Quin leaned his head down to her level, folding himself almost in half. "I don't think that's helping."

"Nope." I popped the P. "Making me feel worse, actually."

Zeus came through my front door, his hair sticking up in all directions. He nodded at Bacon and then speared his fingers along his scalp, revealing how his normal hairstyle got so mussed. "What do we know?"

"I need a bigger house."

Everyone's eyes swung to me and I shrugged. My brain wasn't quite up to firing on all cylinders, preferring to keep to safer subjects than the vision of Drym, completely limp as four men in all black tactical gear stuffed him into the back of a van.

Worrying about how if just two wyrfangs crowded my small apartment, it'd never be able to hold all six, was much better territory.

Cavi gave a more appropriate answer after they stared at me for longer than was comfortable.

"They used a drone. Sedative darts followed by nets subdued him."

His eyes flicked to me.

"He surrendered without a fight. We learned long ago to save our strength for the opening they will eventually give him."

I was shaking my head. "No, we aren't waiting. We're going after him." I flopped onto the couch and started pulling my boots on.

"We planned for this outcome, Kendal."

Zeus was using his 'calm down little lady' voice and I was having none of it.

"You planned for them knowing about the meeting? No. You didn't. The fae was just supposed to see him. This was an ambush! How did they know to set it up? How were they ready with a god damn drone?"

Everyone's eyes swung from me to Zeus.

"Aymar knew about them, and that they'd escaped. When I contacted him, he guessed I was going to tell him about them, so he told his superiors about the meet." He shook his head.

"Since the wyrfangs' existence was kept secret, the only way I could have known about them was if I'd seen one or been told about them. They sent the team, in the hopes I'd lead them to you. I should have known better, but it doesn't matter now. What's done is done."

"We're going in and getting him."

His heavy hand fell on my shoulder and I shrugged it off, not wanting anyone to touch me.

"Yes, we are. But not tonight. He needs time to gather information we need."

I crossed my arms over my chest. "How much time?"

Zeus looked at Cavi, who looked at Quin, who rolled his eyes. "He asked for a week."

"A week?"

Even Bacon winced at my screech.

"Fuck no. I'm not going to sit around for a week while he's in some hell site of a lab being tortured."

"They won't torture him." Everyone looked at Cavi. "They'll want to capture us all before we're punished." His voice dropped. "They'll want us to see each other in pain. To drive home the hopelessness of another escape attempt."

"Well that's not fucking happening! It's bad enough they got Drym. They aren't getting the rest of you." I jumped up and stomped across my living room and back, every other step a heavy *clomp* since I'd only managed to get one boot on.

I poked my index finger into the hard muscle of Zeus's chest. "And how did this happen, anyway? I thought your contact was supposed to come alone."

He rubbed at his abused pec. "He did. They followed him. He was just as shocked as we were. Probably because he fears repercussions. The fae won't take kindly to him sharing secrets outside class."

"Well, at least we know a fae is definitely in cahoots with BioSynth." I sat back down, sinking into the well-worn back of my hand-me-down couch. "What do we do now?"

"You're going to hate it."

I cut my eyes at Cavi. "I already do."

"We wait." Zeus held up a hand before I could protest. "And we prepare. I need to bring in a couple of specialized team members to confer with Kragen and the rest of the wyrfangs.

"In the interim, I think I can solve at least one problem."

"Oh, which one is that?" I side-eyed the werewolf.

"The one regarding your apartment being too small. Bull found what looks to be a perfect property. We just need your and the brothers' approval before we sign the contract."

"Finally, some good news." I perked up and shoved on my other boot. I was at the door before I noticed they weren't following me. "What are we waiting for?" I snapped my fingers. "Real estate waits for no man. Or woman. Or wyrfang."

KENZIE KELLY

THIRTY-FOUR

I FELT NOTHING BUT the cold concrete floor of the cell they locked me in. I still feigned sleep, but that trick wouldn't work much longer. It was hard enough to stay limp while the guards manhandled me into this building.

I sat up and shook like I was just waking up from the drug. We had done a good job of destroying the lab when we escaped, but they'd managed to build a new one faster than we anticipated.

There was no creativity in the layout. I was in the second to most left-hand cell of six. Two cameras positioned inside the cell, and another dozen scattered around the exterior area, kept their unblinking eyes pinned on me.

There was a large observation window that spanned across the room opposite the cells. It appeared to be a mirror, but was one-way glass. I wondered if the director stood there now, watching me.

My cell was empty. No bed, no sink, no toilet. I hadn't expected any. We only got such luxuries after a good mission. They were often taken away soon after for some imagined infraction.

I sank on my haunches and put my back against the wall. I rested my head on my crossed arms and stared at the line of shifting pinpoints of light. They were strong and steady. I had no fresh pain in my body.

Kendal was safe.

I'm sure by now my brothers had told her the plan for if I was captured. She would be mad as hell. I was glad we couldn't feel each other's emotions.

As calm as I seemed on the outside, I couldn't deny that being back under the thumb of scientists scared the shit out of me. It was worse now. I knew what they were capable of, and instead of believing that's how everything was, I had experienced freedom. Kindness. Hope.

Love.

I'm not sure when I fell in love with Kendal, but I was pretty sure it was soon after she fell into my legs that first night. The confusion I felt when such a small thing caused such big emotions to riot through me should have given me a clue. The aggression and need to keep her safe—even from my brothers—was another sign.

I held myself back, not wanting to pressure her into a lifetime of being with a monster. Especially after reading Bacon's information that shifter bonds are for life.

When she ran from me, her sparkling eyes and squeals of laughter when I caught her made it undeniable. My heart was hers. My body hers to command. My soul hers to do with as she wished.

I loved my brothers, but the depth of feeling I had for Kendal went far beyond that.

I had to get out of here.

And I could only do that when I had the information we needed. The concrete proof a fae was working with a human on illegal experiments against the council's wishes. That they planned to stage a coup.

I didn't know how I was going to get it, but I knew I only had a week. That was the time we'd agreed on. They would give me one week to find what I could, and then my brothers and the entirety of Superhuman Security were coming for me.

The single door to the outer lab slid open. A scientist clipped into the room. Her heels beat a staccato rhythm on the concrete floor. She stopped so close to the front of my cell that when she turned to the side, her clipboard banged into it. Her long, straight brown hair pulled at her face from the severe bun at the nape of her neck, giving her a stretched look.

My jaw fell open before I snapped it shut. The last person I imagined seeing here, dressed in a white lab coat, with credentials snapped to the breast pocket, was Isabelle Blackwell.

She should be in hiding. She helped us escape, after all.

My ears popped and I shook. She spoke quickly. The glamour she'd put over the two of us wouldn't last long.

"I'm sorry. I pretended to be a victim. I never imagined they'd capture one of you." Her eyes darted to the cameras at the corners of my cell. "I had to stay with BioSynth. I knew they'd continue their research, with or without you. I've been searching for proof, the identities of the major stakeholders—anything I can expose them with."

"Have you found it?"

"No. Not yet."

"We will search together."

She nodded and I could feel the pressure in my ears lessening.

Before her spell faded completely, she blurted, "Roul?"

"As well as expected."

She cringed, so I knew she understood. No, he wasn't doing well at all. He saw her refusal to come with us as a betrayal, but it wasn't. It would be good to see them reunited.

Her voice changed, her tone clipped and professional as she barked commands. "Stand and turn."

I was slow to follow her directions, but I followed them.

To the room at large she cataloged me like a prize possession.

"Subject two appears in good health and condition. No obvious wounds. Scales and fur bright and shiny. Eyes glowing appropriately." She tapped her pen against the side of the clipboard. "Open your mouth."

I dropped my jaw, adding a growl to my performance for those who watched.

"Teeth intact."

Without another word, she left. It was deathly silent. I was the only living thing inside this soundproofed room. My heart pined for Kendal. I focused on our bond; the lights pulsing at my attention. I hope she saw them flicker. I hope she knew I was sending her love and comfort.

I felt neither of those things. For the first time in my life, I was alone. Loneliness was a miserable emotion.

THIRTY-FIVE

OUR BOND LIGHTS PULSED and somehow I knew it was Drym. He was okay. I relaxed a fraction and let myself take in the majesty in front of me.

The property was a small preserve not far outside Damruck. A gravel road sliced through the middle of dense forest and ended at a long structure that was used for gatherings.

The inside was dusty and stagnant from disuse, but the windows along both sides were functional. A giant fireplace stood at the opposite end. There was enough room inside for all six wyrfangs to be comfortable, plus quite a few other supernaturals and (I hoped one day) humans.

The floors were beautiful, wide plank heart pine. I could easily envision what a good cleaning and a coat of paint would do.

It was perfect.

"Are there any houses?"

Zeus shook his head. "No, but there are building sites already mapped and perk tested. I thought each of them would want to choose their floor plan and architecture style."

"That's probably wise. We'll need to give them options. The sheer number of house plans available would be overwhelming. Maybe three options in each style? They can narrow them down from there."

"So, you approve?"

"I very much approve. I'm not sure how we'll afford this, though."

"Like I said before, the council will foot the bill, and what they don't cover, I will. We take care of our own."

I nearly sagged in relief. It was a dream come true in a lot of ways. Plenty of land for the 'fangs to run and be free. The ability to choose whichever house plan suited each of their needs and personalities. Far enough off the beaten path to not be bothered, but close enough to let me go to town when I needed.

I spun a slow circle until I faced Zeus again. I grinned. "We'll take it." Then I gasped and threw my hand over my mouth. "I mean, one sec!" I skipped outside with a giddy smile. "So… what do you think, guys?"

The five of them looked at each other. Kragen spoke for them. "Do you think it's appropriate? Do you think it will fit our needs?"

I nodded. "Yes, I do."

"Then we agree. We have no frame of reference for these things. We trust you Kendal."

Four words that made my eyes leak. I wasn't sure anyone had said they trusted me before. My parents certainly didn't, rest their souls. Don't get me wrong, I loved them, but they expected a rebellious daughter and I wasn't. I got good grades and always made curfew. They still questioned me about where I was and who I was with.

It didn't matter that I led a very boring life during my teen and young adult years. It wasn't until after they were killed in a car accident that I let myself loose a bit. I spent a good year getting tipsy every night in bars across town. The seedier the better.

Until I got sick of being hungover every day.

I'd like to think I reached a happy middle. I was no monk, but I wasn't hanging out with biker gangs anymore either.

I guess instead of motorcycles and leather my tastes had changed to fur and horns.

Thurl put his hand tentatively on my shoulder. His ears drooped and he whined. "Why are you sad, Kendal?"

"I'm not sad, I'm happy. These are happy tears."

He looked at his brothers, his head cocking. "This place makes you happy?"

I shook my head. "No, you make me happy. It's been a while since I've had friends who cared about me. Even longer since I've had a family."

Quin, Cavi and Thurl tilted their heads back and howled. Kragen had an indulgent smile on his face.

"What's happening?"

"You make us happy, too. These are happy howls."

My tears didn't stop, even through a burst of laughter. Thurl picked me up and twirled me around before almost throwing me down and backing away. "Sorry."

I swiped at the tears on my cheeks. "It's okay."

Bull appeared from somewhere, his tall lanky frame and habit of going everywhere with a laptop not hampering his ability to move without sound. Though the 'fangs heard him, their heads swiveling like a school of fish.

"Our offer has been accepted and they're willing to close immediately. Apparently the property has sat vacant long enough they're just happy to be rid of it." He held the laptop in the palm of his left hand, his eyes glued to the screen, his right hand typing away. He finally looked up after a few minutes.

"We'll need to send a representative to the closing. Who wants to stand as proxy for the wyrfang?"

Kragen stepped up. "Kendal should go."

Zeus swung his head in that direction. "Whoever goes will sign the paperwork to gain ownership of the property. One of my team members can stand in using one of your new identities."

I laid my hand on Kragen's forearm, and it tensed beneath my fingers. It reminded me how they were unused to affectionate touch and my heart broke for them. I decided to hug them each once a day.

"Kragen, I appreciate that you're offering to put me on the deed, and I'll go if you want that, but you or one of your brothers should also be on it. Then you can officially name beneficiaries, so if something were to happen to one of you, the others wouldn't have to worry about their homes being taken away."

"Couldn't you make us your beneficiary?" He stumbled over the unfamiliar word.

I nodded. "I could, I suppose?" I looked at Zeus for confirmation. I'd never owned anything worth assigning a beneficiary before.

"Yes. That would work. In the eyes of Society's council, you and Drym are bonded, so you've automatically become the inheritor of each other's property. It's the normal's rules and regulations that can prove tricky sometimes. We have a fae lawyer who can navigate the complexities later."

"Well then." I dusted my hands on my jeans. "I'll sign the paperwork. While I'm doing that, Zeus, can you show the 'fangs each of the housing sites so they can decide who will be where?"

"Of course."

As I slid into the passenger side of Bull's SUV, the joy of the successful property expedition faded. The bond lights floated around my head and stretched into the distance. *I hope you're okay.* I scanned my body for any new aches and pains and there were none, but I still couldn't shake the feeling that the beast I loved was in a miserable place with awful people.

And I couldn't do anything to help him.

THIRTY-SIX

THOUGHTS OF KENDAL KEPT me from spiraling into a well of self-pity. That and Isabelle's sporadic visits were the only things breaking the monotony of life inside the laboratory.

She told me during one visit that my presence had provided enough of a distraction that her search for damning evidence sped up considerably.

At least there was one good thing about my capture.

They had yet to open my cell for any reason, which meant I wasn't able to help her at all. I knew Kendal was safe with my brothers beyond the reach of these scientists, but Isabelle was undercover in the thick of them. I worried for her. If something happened to her, Roul would go mad.

Thurl was already so shy and reserved that he was almost feral. I couldn't lose another brother to brooding withdrawal.

Roul was heartbroken when she disappeared after our escape. My brothers and I stopped asking if he wanted to look for her when his disposition kept getting worse. I knew the hurt he felt was overwhelming. Especially since none of us knew why she refused to come with us.

Now I knew. She never really left us. She was trying to protect us the only way she knew how—by going back into BioSynth undercover. Literally risking her life.

Whether or not we had proof, when I got out of here she was going with me. I wouldn't risk my brother's happiness.

She had to be his mate. He behaved with her the same way I did with Kendal.

Kendal.

Her face was etched in my memory, the smell of her seemed to fill my nostrils and the taste of her flooded my mouth with saliva.

I heard the outer door slide open, but didn't raise my head. A sour, burnt smell pushed Kendal's sweet scent from my nose and made me irrationally angry. I looked up, surprised to see a single man.

They usually came in pairs or packs.

HELD BY A MONSTER

I guessed he was late middle-aged, judging by the gray in his hair and mustache. Thin-framed glasses sat low on his nose, making me wonder if they were needed or just an attempt to appear smarter.

Though not overly heavy, he seemed doughy. Soft everywhere. The sleeves of his dress shirt were rolled up to his elbows, revealing overly hairy forearms. His lips pressed into a thin line.

"You have cost me a lot of time and money with the foolish attempt at running away."

I stood to my full height and got close enough to the barrier between us that my breath fogged the glass.

"Do you expect me to apologize?"

He didn't shrink back or flinch. This was a man who held actual power. Who went through the world believing himself to be invincible because of the influence and money he held.

He snorted. "No. I didn't breed you to be weak. I do, however, expect you to tell me where the rest are. Their swift retrieval will spare you and them considerable pain."

It was then that it dawned on me that his shirt was blue, his slacks and shoes neat and polished. This was Mr. Blue.

"Do you know they call you Mr. Blue?"

That widened his eyes. He quickly recovered. "Who?"

"All of Society that knows about you." I curled my hands into fists, letting my claws sink into my palms so I didn't strike out. We'd learned long ago that it was useless. The walls that contained us were several thicknesses of bulletproof glass. We'd all broken a claw trying to get through it.

"So you found Society." He sighed and *clucked* his tongue. "I wish you hadn't done that, but it speaks to the intelligence and strategy we bred into you. It does make our operation more complicated, but nothing our partners can't handle."

"You mean the fae council member who is working with you?"

That stiffened his muscles. I could almost see the gears of his mind working behind his eyes. Trying to figure out how much we knew and how we'd gained the information so fast.

I hoped spilling that little of what we knew would get him to make a mistake. The need to deny was usually strong among powerful humans when they'd been caught.

When he simply smirked and left I upgraded the amount of threat I thought he posed. This man was no stranger to shady deals and navigating deeper waters. To so easily dismiss what we had uncovered, he must be powerful indeed.

Only a few minutes after he left, Isabelle appeared. My ears popped as she came toward me. She was grinning.

"I don't know what you said to him, but boy, is he pissed! He's in his office right now yelling at someone so loud that the entire floor can hear him."

"I'm glad he's more rattled than he appeared."

"Oh yeah, you definitely shook him. Everybody is trying to scatter before they become an easy target for his anger. I'm going to use his focus on whatever went wrong to search his office."

"What? You can't do that. You'll be caught."

"No, I won't. Nobody dares to go in there when he hasn't invited them. I heard him call for his helicopter, so as soon as he's left the building I'll slip in and out. Easy peasy, lemon squeezy."

"Easy ... what?"

She shook her head and brought her clipboard up as my ears popped again. She made a couple of check marks on the paper, winked at me, and left.

My skin itched and I flexed my hands as I paced. I didn't like her idea. There were too many unknowns, too many risks. My ears swiveled as I searched for any sign of alarm. Time passed slower than before with nothing to do but worry.

I slid down the back wall, rested on my haunches, and focused on the bond lights. They were still strong, still danced happily in the air between me and the door that locked me away from my mate.

I counted my breaths, cracks in the floor tiles, the number of times the cameras whirled to life—anything to distract me from what might be happening on the other side of the door.

All sound ceased with a snap, and I plunged into darkness.

Isabelle's distorted voice said, "Get ready to move."

I crept toward the door to my cell, staying low. The last time she'd cast such a powerful spell, all the cell doors had opened and we'd been freed. This time was no different. The door slid open and sound rushed in.

I heard the clicking with just enough time to move to the side. The outer door blew inward, so close I felt the breeze it caused as it flew past.

A man with dark, swept back hair and an unhinged grin stepped in. I recognized him as Wasp—one of Zeus's people.

"Hello! This is your rescue." He bowed low and swept an arm from me to the outside. "If you'll please step this way. Hurry now, they're bound to have heard that." He chuckled.

I shook my head and followed him down a long corridor. Red lights flashed overhead and people ran panicked from one room to another, trailing papers like slug trails.

The man stuck his hand out at me. "I'm Wasp, explosives ordinance for Superhuman Security. Zeus says 'hi'!"

"I remember." I looked at his hand, and then my own fingers tipped with claws. I waved.

He grinned. "Right, probably a better idea."

"Isabelle?"

"She sent up the bat signal when she found proof linking the director of BioSynth to the fae councilman. I'd been standing by, waiting for the chance to blow something up."

"Is she safe?"

He glanced over at me. "I can't say. Her last communique was that the job wasn't done, and she'd resurface when she knew more."

"Fuck." Roul was going to go mad.

Wasp shrugged. "Witches are unpredictable, but solid. I'm sure she'll be fine."

I smelled grass and water before we turned the corner and stepped through a hole that was blasted in the wall. The back door of an SUV with blacked-out windows opened and Kendal's head popped out.

"Get in!"

THIRTY-SEVEN

DRYM DOVE INTO THE vehicle and crushed me to his chest. "What are you doing here?"

I squeezed him as hard as I could and pressed my ear to his pec. Hearing the steady beat of his heart let me breathe. "We were the closest vehicle when Wasp called for exfil. Bull wanted to keep going and let someone else come, but I convinced him otherwise."

From the driver's seat, Bull called out, "As in, she pulled a gun on me."

"It worked, didn't it?"

Drym's arms pulsed around me. "You should have listened. You could have been hurt."

"Me? I could have been hurt?" I pulled back and poked him. "You were captured by mad scientists. I've gone crazy thinking about what they were doing to you in there! No way was I going to make you wait one more second if I could help it."

The SUV hit a pothole and Drym pulled me onto his lap. "You would have felt it if they'd hurt me."

"Don't use logic. This is no time for logic." I wrapped my hand around his muzzle and pulled his head down so I could look into his eyes. "Four days, Drym. You were in there for four days."

He licked my forearm, the two sides of his tongue trailing up the sides of my wrist. "I missed you."

"Don't think I don't know what you're doing. You're distracting me. I'm going to let it work because I missed you, too."

I snaked my arms around his neck and leaned into him. He ran his claws through my hair, careful not to scrape my scalp.

"I'm going to have Cavi remove my claws."

I sat back. "Absolutely not. I found a solution, and they'll arrive in a day or two."

He flicked one ear back. "What is it?"

"You'll see." I smiled at his grunt.

Bull pulled into the gravel drive and Drym's ears perked. "Where are we going?"

HELD BY A MONSTER

I grinned. "Y'all have new digs. The sleeping arrangements are temporary, but construction starts on Kragen and Cavi's houses next week."

I hopped out when Bull stopped in front of what we'd dubbed the common hall. It was still the only structure on the property, but not for long. One wall had pallets, piles of blankets, and one blow-up mattress spaced along it. I couldn't convince any of them to get mattresses, but I hoped they'd come around.

We all moved in as soon as the paperwork was finished. I didn't want to be too far from Drym's brothers, just in case something else went wrong and they had to rescue him early.

The day after I signed the paperwork, I followed our bond lights until we came to a locked and guarded gate. I pointed out where Drym was inside the low-slung, gray, concrete block building. They wanted me to go home after that, but I no longer felt like my apartment was home.

The long, live edge wooden table that served as a centerpiece in the cave now stood in the middle of the common room. One end was scattered with laptops and the other held stacks of blueprints.

The brothers rushed forward and surrounded Drym. They didn't hug, but Kragen put a hand on his shoulder.

"You are unharmed?"

"Yes. It was strange. Only two scientists and the one I assume is Mr. Blue entered. They took standard readings and asked standard questions, but I think they were hoping I'd give up your location. I managed to unnerve Mr. Blue, and the lab became a blur of activity, but I was on my way out with Wasp by then."

Kragen nodded. "Our contact on the inside confirmed they were hoping to use threats of violence against us to persuade you to divulge our location."

I caught Kragen's slight tilt in Roul's direction. Drym told me in the car that Isabelle stayed embedded with BioSynth, and that she had never left. She was still trying to root out every evil tendril of the company.

I wasn't sure if Roul would appreciate knowing she hadn't abandoned him, or if he would be more heartbroken that she wouldn't give up the pursuit.

We all turned toward the door as Zeus, Bull, and Wasp entered. Zeus clapped Drym on the back.

"Good to have you back."

Drym dipped his nose and pushed me a step away from Wasp.

The smart dressed man just laughed. "I think I scare him."

"Your enthusiasm for explosives doesn't inspire a great deal of confidence in your mental stability."

HELD BY A MONSTER

I shoved at Drym. "That's rude."

Bull barked out a laugh. "But totally accurate."

An entirely unrepentant Wasp shrugged.

Bull set up his laptop in the only space that remained on the table. "We've had a cursory look at the data your insider sent. Both BioSynth and the fae have done a good job covering their tracks and their asses. Mr. Blue—whose real name is Robert Willis—has an operating agreement with the normals government, and a writ of sanction from the fae council."

"He didn't flinch." Drym's growl was low.

"What's that?" Zeus asked.

"Willis didn't flinch when I revealed that we'd unearthed his secrets. I knew then he was dangerously powerful. That he feels untouchable."

"Those two endorsements are certainly why. Even if brought before the entire Society council, he could say he thought the fae were speaking on their behalf. No one in normal government would dare question him."

Zeus and Bull shared a look. "I think it's time for the full council to meet the wyrfangs."

THIRTY-EIGHT

"I'M GOING WITH you."

I'd taken Kendal outside and we walked silently deep into the woods. I tried to prepare arguments against her statement, but I couldn't seem to think of any.

The truth was, I wanted her by my side.

I nodded. "Of course."

She stopped and stared up at me. "I thought you'd fight it."

I carefully cupped her cheeks in my palms. "Unless the risk is too great, I want you with me, always."

Zeus, Bull, and Wasp left hours ago. Society council's next meeting was in two days. Enough time for me to see the building site Kendal picked for us, and explore our new home.

It was surreal. This property, this haven, was ours. We would pay Zeus back as we could by helping him with cases which called for our unique talents. Zeus assured us he needed no payment, but we wouldn't feel right not giving back.

Even now security fencing was going up around the perimeter of the preserve. The fence kept humans out, but allowed wildlife to roam freely. The forest behind Kendal's apartment wasn't even half the size of this one.

I'd spent most my life in a small, translucent box, being watched. No privacy. No autonomy.

Freedom was overwhelming.

Kragen and Cavi adjusted well. Quin masked every emotion with a hefty dose of humor, so it was hard to tell what his true feelings were. Thurl and Roul struggled. Their singular purpose was aggression. They both were learning a new way of living. It wouldn't be an easy transition for them.

That night I would tell Roul about Isabelle. Zeus cautioned against it, but my brothers and I didn't keep secrets. Whether it helped or caused further hurt was yet to be seen. Either way, we would stand beside him.

Going from captivity to this wide-open space was jarring. I expected at any moment for it to be taken away. Nets to fall from the sky, tranquilizer darts to fly from all directions. I knew it would take time for it to feel real. Even longer for it to feel safe.

HELD BY A MONSTER

I hoped Kendal would ease my way.

It might be unfair to put such a burden on her.

"I rely on you, perhaps too much."

Her brows came together. "What do you mean?"

"I see you as a lifeline. As a tether to the reality of freedom and safety."

She wrapped both arms around me and pressed her cheek to my chest. "You are my lifeline, too. You rescued me and have kept me safe." Her inhale shuddered. "You are my home."

I nuzzled her neck and she giggled.

"Cold nose."

I swiped my tongue along the curve of her collarbone, up to trace her jaw. She sighed and leaned into me.

"No one's around, right? None of the others are close?"

I tilted my head and listened. "No, they aren't close."

"Good." She grabbed the hem of her shirt and pulled it over her head, then pushed her pants and underwear down. She shimmied out of her bra and stood naked in front of me, like a wood nymph queen.

"You are stunning." I whispered with reverence as I stalked closer. "I am not worthy of your affections."

"But you have them, anyway."

She ran her hands up my belly and back down, gripping my swollen cock.

"I don't know which 'parent' gave you these spikes, but I need to send them a fruit basket or something."

She bent at the waist and sucked my tip into her mouth. I managed to strangle out "dragon," before speech became impossible.

I buried my claws in the nearest tree to keep from sinking to the ground as her mouth worked magic. I watched as the tip of her tongue flicked the spiraling row of short spikes, sending repeated zings of pleasure through me.

It was a delicious sort of torture.

I was vibrating with the need to sink myself into her.

I succumbed to the impulse and lay her back on the ground. She gasped when I shoved my nose between her thighs, bathing my muzzle in her honeysuckle scent and lapping at her entrance.

She writhed and moaned as I worked her until I nipped at her clit and she cried out.

I watched the walls of her pussy clench.

"So greedy."

She made a soft noise as she came down from her orgasm, which turned into a moan as I pushed inside. Her warm heat wrapped my cock and sent my eyes rolling in my head.

"I'm not sure I can be gentle."

She grabbed my nose and pulled my eyes to hers. "Good. I want my monster to fuck me. I want to feel that you're here, safe, with me."

I trembled with the depth of emotion coursing through my veins. I loved this woman more than life itself. I had killed for her, and would again. My entire world was this small, soft female, urging me faster with her heels.

I couldn't get close enough, deep enough, to satisfy my need to possess, to mark, to leave no doubt that she belonged to me.

I sank my claws into the earth on either side of her head, careful to keep the sharp tips away from her as I pounded her body.

I came with a roar and gathered her into my arms. When I'd caught my breath, I sighed into her ear, "I cannot lose you."

She squeezed her arms around my neck. "I can't lose you either."

"I will eliminate every threat against you."

"I will stand at your side while you do it."

I felt her smile against the ruff of my fur. "Let's tear these assholes down."

THIRTY-NINE

DRYM AND I SLEPT in the clearing where our house would be built. Surrounded by him, warm and safe cuddled on his chest, it was easy to pretend the danger was over. I smiled as I pushed through the door into the common hall.

Halfway to the table, I stumbled to a stop. All six of the 'fangs gathered at the far end in a loose circle, their muscles stiff with tension. Roul stood in the center, his eyes shut and his hands clenched into tight fists.

The others murmured in low voices. I couldn't hear what they were saying, but it was obvious they were trying to calm and soothe.

I cocked my head in question when Drym glanced back at me.

He shook his head and flicked his nose at me, wordlessly telling me to get out.

I hesitated until Roul opened his eyes, tilted his head back and roared. The amount of pain and anger in that sound made me retreat. They had told him about Isabelle. It was the only thing that made sense. I wondered if it was the right thing to do, but what's done was done.

Seeing me might mean more pain, so I left. My heart broke for him. I understood why Isabelle did what she did, but it would be hard for him not to feel abandoned.

It wasn't long before Drym stepped out and came to where I sat in the SUV the shifters left for us.

"He is lost in the fog."

"The fog?"

Drym looked away and his ears drooped. "In times of high emotion or stress, we enter a state we call the fog. Our focus narrows to a single point, a single objective. Survive, by any means. Nothing else registers."

He sighed. "It makes us unpredictable, uncontrollable, and dangerous to everyone near."

"How long will he be in this fog?"

"I'm not sure, but I would rather you not be here for a while."

I nodded. "Okay, I'll go into town. I think I have a package to pick up, anyway."

He leaned into the car and hugged me. I buried my face in the fur of his neck and inhaled.

"Be careful, Kendal."

"I will."

He released a shuddering exhale and made his way back inside.

The drive into Damruck took me winding through pines and fields freshly plowed, waiting to be planted. I sang along to the latest pop songs at the top of my lungs, feeling better than I had in weeks.

Drym was back safe. The gentle glow of our bond lights seemed to dance along with me. I pulled into a shopping center with a locally owned coffee shop and treated myself to a latte and a decadent chocolate croissant.

My next stop was the post office. When I'd moved out of my apartment, I opened a box since the wyrfang compound didn't have a mailbox yet. I was giddy to find the package notice and grinned like a deranged villain when I took it from the worker.

I opened it and squealed when I was back in the car. My friend had come through for me, big time. They were perfect. I packed them back into the box and decided to make one last stop before I went home.

I walked out of the store balancing the tray of twenty-four cupcakes on my forearm as I dug into my purse for the keys. I hoped the sugary goodness would distract Roul for a second or two.

At the SUV, I set them on the hood and told myself for the umpteenth time I needed a smaller purse.

I didn't see the three men until they surrounded me. I spun to run, but one wrapped an arm around my waist and pushed a cloth over my nose and mouth. A van pulled up, the side door sliding open.

Adrenaline rushed through me and I fought with everything I had, only it wasn't much. My limbs were sluggish, my thoughts slow, and my eyes lost focus.

I remember the sharp pain of my shin hitting the edge of the van's door just before I sank into darkness.

FORTY

I SUCKED IN A breath as a knife drew across my shin. I bent to inspect my leg, but there was nothing there.

Kendal.

I bolted outside, but the clearing in front of the common house was empty. Our bond lights stretched into the distance, but before I could take off on all fours, Kragen's hand wrapped around my arm.

"What's wrong?"

I jerked out of his hold. "Something happened to Kendal."

I could hear my brothers shouting at me as I dropped to all fours and tore off, following the pulsing lights that would lead me to my mate.

FORTY-ONE

I BLINKED MY EYES open and stared, trying to figure out where I was and what had happened. They kidnapped me. Again. The memory of being shoved into the van came back in a rush and I sat up in a panic.

I regretted it immediately. My head swam like I'd spent all night doing my best to drink a distillery. I whimpered and dropped back on the couch.

I heard a door open and close, then the creak of a chair as someone sat nearby.

"I've set some water in front of you. Move slowly. They gave you a sedative for easier transport, but they overdid the dosing a bit."

"Where? Who?" My brain had taken a vacation and my mouth felt like I'd tried to eat a package of cotton balls.

The chair squeaked again and I drew my five-hundred-pound eyelids up. Mr. Blue, aka Robert Willis, sat in a cheap folding chair like it was a throne. His legs were stretched in front of him, his arms crossed over his chest, a signature blue tie revealing his identity.

He cocked his head at me. "We've met." A small smile spread across his thin lips, making him look like a cartoon.

I snorted. "Of course. The man who enjoys hunting women in the woods."

He shrugged. "One of many pastimes." He looked around the small room. "As for where, that doesn't matter. I suspect we won't be here long."

I inched my way to an upright position and grabbed the bottle of water off the floor. I drank half of it while I scanned my surroundings. The room looked like it was once an office. A long window looked out over an expanse of concrete a story below. At one point, this must have been a manufacturing facility of some sort, but now it was an empty shell.

I sat on a couch that was ripped in multiple places, with its stuffing poking through and its useful life as furniture clearly over long ago. There was nothing else in the room.

My arms were too heavy to support the water bottle for long and I let them drop into my lap. "So, Robert, what now?" I emphasized his name. I wanted him to know I knew who he was. I was probably signing my own death warrant, but at that point I was so mad I didn't care.

If he was surprised, he didn't show it. Drym was right. This man didn't flinch.

"Now we wait for my wayward squad to come rescue you."

He chuckled at my confusion.

"Imagine my surprise when my staff informed me that the key to getting back an extravagant investment was the same woman who escaped my hunt. It makes sense now, how you disappeared that night. When the dogs lost your trail we assumed you'd fallen into an old well or another such hazard. Then you showed up at your apartment.

"We had to send men after you, of course. It wouldn't do for our little side hobby to be spoken about. But you eluded them, too. I should have known when they disappeared without a trace."

He shook his head and *tsked* as though he admonished himself for not seeing it sooner.

"A-546 never said a word while we had him. Did you know that?"

I kept silent.

"I knew he wouldn't give up the location of the others, and one subject isn't enough to command the price I need to make this project worthwhile. I need the entire squad."

He glanced at his watch. It was one of those high-tech ones, the square face displaying much more than the time.

My brain finally processed what he was saying. I was bait. This was a trap. And knowing Drym, it would work.

I had to figure out a way to stop him from coming.

Robert checked his watch again. "It was simple enough to insert a tracker while he was down. Harder to make it seem like the shifter's escape plan wasn't too easy." He sighed. "We didn't expect their hiding place to be so secure."

I kept quiet. I didn't want to interrupt him when he was engrossed in his villain speech.

"After you slipped through our fingers a second time, I decided to let you go."

I snorted.

"I promise you, Kendal. We explored every avenue to retrieving the wyrfangs without involving you, but this was our best course."

"They will kill you all."

His thin lips spread into that evil grin again.

"Not with you as an incentive to ensure their cooperation."

He glanced at his watch and stood. "Drink your water. They will be here soon and I need to show them that behaving results in your good care."

The insinuation that misbehaving resulted in bad treatment of me hung in the air.

"I see you understand. Good." The door clicked shut behind him.

Think Kendal, think. There has to be a way to warn them.

I dropped my head into my hands and my eyes snagged on the bloody scrape slashed across my leg. I laid my forearm across my thighs and took a deep breath. Then I scratched a word into my skin, over and over, and hoped like hell he figured it out.

KENZIE KELLY

FORTY-TWO

I SLID TO A stop just inside the tree line around the warehouse. I had to be smart about this. I needed to ensure Kendal wasn't hurt while I rescued her.

The building was dark. The parking lot around it cracked from the weeds that struggled to survive in the tiny spaces where dirt met air.

The side facing me held a small door. The glass of its small window was smashed, but the wire between the panes still held the last of the shards.

My right ear flicked back as my brothers slid to a stop behind me. They fanned out in a line, Kragen on my right and Roul to my left. My head swung left first, but Roul's focus never wavered from the warehouse.

Kragen shook his head. "It's a trap, Drym."

"I know." For the past few minutes, the word 'trap' scratched across the skin of my forearm. My sweet, beautiful mate was warning me.

"We should call in the shifters."

I swung my head to our de facto leader. "We don't need them."

He shook his head. "No, but their presence might make Willis think twice about his plan.

"Not with his two get out of jail free cards, as Bull called them."

"We don't know what waits for us inside."

I growled, low in my throat. "My mate waits for us." I sat back on my haunches. "But we can't approach this without a plan."

Kragen took a deep breath. "We need intel. We need to know the size and location of the force inside."

I dipped my nose. "We need Zeus."

Roul's heavy hand landed on my shoulder. "They are on their way. Cavi and Quin, wait for them at the road."

The tips of his claws dug into me and earned my attention.

"If you feel her being hurt, we will not wait."

HELD BY A MONSTER

I nodded, even though everything inside me roared. My mate was a few hundred yards away. No cell in my body wanted to wait.

FORTY-THREE

MY HEAD DROPPED BACK against the couch cushion. After finishing the water, I'd laid back down. The room still spun, but it had slowed down. I had to believe my message had been received. I couldn't hear a commotion, and the warehouse floor was just as empty as I first saw it.

Our bond lights bunched tightly together. Drym was close, but waiting. The 'fangs were bred for this, raised for this. I trusted they knew what they were doing.

A loud knock reverberated through the building. The world seemed to stop and hold its breath.

I heard Robert outside my door and hurried to press my ear against the metal.

"Of course you open it, idiot. They've figured out the situation and we can only assume they're surrendering."

I bit my cheek to keep from laughing as the saying about assuming things ran through my head.

I went back to the observation window and saw two figures moving through the gloom to a spot underneath me. The window faced a set of large, rolltop doors, so I guessed the walk-through door was beneath this office.

For a few seconds, all was quiet.

Then the entire space lit up as a wide river of flame swept from one side of the floor to the other. I didn't have time to wonder where they managed to get a flamethrower, since the door to the office was flung open and Robert hurried inside.

Screams seemed to ring out from every direction, the sound pinging off the metal walls.

I smiled as Robert rushed across the room, yanked me in front of him and anchored me to his chest with an arm.

I nearly gagged being so close to him. Instead of Drym's hard muscles and soft fur, I felt like I sank into a marshmallow. I pushed against his hold until I felt the cold steel of a gun barrel press into my temple.

"I'll kill you if I must, so stay still."

"Coward," I hissed.

"I prefer the term realist. I know what I created, and I have no chance of winning against them if they make their way up here."

The man at my back seemed calm, but the gun shook. He was smart to be afraid.

Orange light lit up the room and I wished I could see the floor. Robert held me in the far corner, so all I could see was the glow from the flames and the smoke that drifted in a thick sheet under the ceiling.

I don't know if it was five minutes or thirty, but soon all the noise ceased and the whole place got eerily quiet. I squeezed my eyes shut and prayed to whoever would listen that Drym and his brothers were okay.

I started when the door opened, revealing a man dressed head to toe in tactical gear, his gun held at his side. I felt Robert relax behind me until the man fell forward like a plank of wood, the door slamming shut behind him. Even in the dim light I could see his back was ripped open down the spine.

The gun jammed into my head, and I winced. Robert shuffled us sideways to the window and we both looked out.

The floor was littered with bodies. None of them were large and covered in fur.

Even as he tensed, I relaxed. He might not have flinched before, but he was now. He jerked me around to face the door and we both watched as the tips of five claws punched through the thin metal. The door yanked backward with a screech and disappeared to the side. Roul stepped through.

I grinned and gave him a finger wave.

"Kendal. You are unharmed?"

"I am."

"Your leg?"

"Scraped when they shoved me into the van. Nothing serious."

Roul's eyes swung to the director. "It is still an injury."

The gun pulsed against my temple.

"I'll injure her a lot worse if you and the others don't stand down immediately."

Roul drew himself to his full, impressive height and crossed his arms. He didn't respond.

"Did you hear me? I know you aren't one of the bright ones, but even you have to see that this is an impossible situation for you to win."

His lips drew back in a snarl. "You were arrogant enough to create us. You of all people should know that there is no situation we can't win."

"I will kill her!"

He shoved us forward a step and before I could blink, the gun fell away. I wasted no time sprinting into Roul's open arms.

He caught me and shoved me behind him, but I peeked around his massive body and grinned.

I stepped to the side so Robert could see me. "I told you they would kill you all."

His shoulder was almost separated from his body, the gun useless on the floor. Behind him stood Drym, who had his hand wrapped around the director's throat. I felt stupid for never looking up. The office ceiling was open to the floor below.

"They have only killed me and my men. This is so much bigger than any of you know."

In a low growl next to Robert's ear, Drym said, "Give us time."

Then he drew the tip of a claw across the man's throat and stepped over him as he dropped to the floor. I threw myself at him and he caught me, wrapped his big arms around me and held me tight.

"You are truly unharmed?"

I chuckled in his ruff. "You would know if they'd hurt me."

"A wise woman once told me that times like these weren't for logic."

I wrapped a hand around his muzzle and kissed the end of his nose. "That was an intelligent woman, indeed."

I laughed as he swung me into his arms and carried me down a set of rickety stairs to the warehouse floor. I blinked against the light as he stepped outside, but I could still see the other four wyrfangs and five members of Superhuman Security standing around a group of mercenaries who were on their knees with their hands behind their heads.

Drym joined them. He didn't put me down and I didn't protest. As far as I was concerned, he could hold me until the end of time. Or at least until I needed to pee.

"What happens to them?" I directed my question at no one in particular, but it was Zeus who answered.

"The council will decide."

He shrugged like he didn't care one way or the other, and I found I didn't either. They'd had a hand in keeping Drym and others confined, so they were as guilty as the rest.

"I guess y'all are the ones who brought the flamethrower?"

The shifters looked confused, and then Wasp dissolved into fits of laughter. Even Zeus chuckled.

"What's so funny?"

Zeus shook his head. "We don't own a flamethrower."

FORTY-FOUR

THEY DIDN'T SEEM INCLINED to explain to Kendal, so I did. "They brought a dragon."

Her head fell back against my bicep and she scanned the skies before her face scrunched up. "I can't believe I missed seeing a fucking dragon."

Everyone laughed. Instinctively, I scanned the sky as well, even though I knew the sleek black supernatural had left after we breached the door. Even had we gone through the loading doors, he wouldn't have been able to fit inside.

I didn't wait for the others as I made my way back through the woods to where the shifters left their vehicles. My brothers would help wrangle the surviving men.

I set her gently in the back of the SUV and ran my hands down her limbs. The scrape on her shin looked bad, but she assured me she was fine. I'd still have Quin look at it when we got home.

Her hand tilted my face up and she smiled. "I'm okay, Drym. I knew you would come for me, but I was so scared you wouldn't get my message."

"We knew it was a trap, but the scratching on my arm slowed me enough to not barrel inside without thought or reason." I leaned into her touch. "You cleared the fog."

She ran her hands down my neck and chest. "And now it's over."

My ears flattened against my skull. "No. The scientist who created us still lives. As do many of the others under his command. Willis may have been the military and political frontman, but the research that created us is still out there."

Her smile dropped and my heart broke that I caused it to disappear.

"But those are problems for another day."

She looked up as she ran her hands along the sides of my face, up my forehead, and cupped my ears, gently urging them forward. "Let's go home. I have a surprise for you."

Her eyes went wide. "Oh no, the cupcakes!"

She searched for something over my shoulder.

"We need to go back to the store and get the car I drove."

It took a minute for me to realize she wasn't talking to me. The others had arrived—or at least some of them had. I turned until I could see it was the shifter named Behemoth. He grunted at Kendal, but didn't speak.

Ghost stepped from behind him and bowed low. "I will be happy to drive you. Don't mind my friend here. He only speaks when his mate is nearby."

The big bear shifter punched the wolf in the arm. The other man rubbed at it, but his grin didn't falter.

"The others are still wrapping up, but we can take this one and drive you into town." Ghost waved at the vehicle I'd set Kendal inside.

The bear shifter grunted. "Stay."

"Right. You stay here and help drive the others back."

Driving was a skill we weren't capable of. It was hard enough to get comfortable riding in the back of these large vehicles, but our legs just weren't designed for operating one. And as I demonstrated with my run to this warehouse on the edge of town, we didn't really need them. We were just as fast on all fours, and we could maneuver through woods instead of being restricted to roads.

Kendal backed up as I folded myself next to her on the seat. I buried my nose in her hair and breathed as the adrenaline left me. I pulled her into my lap and she wound her arms around my neck. I didn't think I could ever get her close enough.

She didn't deserve to be bound to a monster like me. I vowed to make every moment of her life the best I could. It would take time to feel secure, for the feeling that she could be ripped away from me at any moment to lessen. That she might come to her senses and leave me.

I knew that feeling would never go away.

"I love you." My words were inadequate to describe the burning feeling in my chest.

"I love you, too." She leaned back suddenly and scanned my chest and arms and an adorable wrinkle appeared between her brows.

"What's wrong?"

"You're clean."

My head tilted to the side. "What?"

"You aren't covered in blood and gore."

I chuckled. "I knew I wouldn't be able to wait to hold you. Given there wasn't a lake nearby, I thought it best to skirt around my brothers and make my way to where you were being held."

She buried her face in my chest. "Smart beast."

Ghost pulled into the store parking lot and stopped next to the SUV Kendal had been driving. She stared out the window.

"I can't believe it's still here. I dropped my purse with the keys. I thought for sure someone would have stolen it."

Ghost turned in the seat to look at us. "Someone in the store saw you get kidnapped. They called 911, who called us when the registration for the car came back to Supe Sec. River went to the station and sorted everything out." He leaned back and handed a key to Kendal. "I brought the spare."

Ghost parked on the passenger side of the other SUV, which made it easy for me to slip from one to the other after Kendal unlocked the door. She closed the door behind me and I heard her thanking Ghost before he sped off.

When she was behind the wheel she leaned into the back seat and reappeared with a small box.

"These are for you."

She was practically vibrating with excitement as I carefully opened the flaps. I managed to pull out a plastic bag holding dozens of… something.

"What are they?" I didn't want to hurt her feelings, but I honestly had no clue what I held.

She took the bag from me and removed one of the things. Then she took my hand in hers and slipped it over the claw of my index finger. I looked from it to her and back again. She rolled her eyes at me and drew my claw down the side of her cheek.

I tried to pull back before I tore her flesh but she was too fast.

"You... aren't hurt."

"Nope!" She shook the bag at me. "These are silicone claw covers. I had a friend make them for you." She looked off into the distance before focusing back on me. "He can make them for the others, if they want them. These are just basic black, but he said he can do just about every color of the rainbow. They aren't permanent, but they dull the points of your claws so you can't hurt me. I mean, you still have to be careful, since your claws can rip through just about anything, but you won't have to be *as* careful as you were."

My jaw hung open. "I can touch you without fear?"

She nodded.

I shoved my hands at her. "Put the rest on."

She laughed at me, but set about covering each of my claws and I couldn't stop the grin that spread across my face.

FORTY-FIVE

THE SOCIETY COUNCIL BUILDING stood just outside downtown. I was surprised they met in Damruck instead of a bigger city, but Zeus explained that Damruck sat on a ley line, which attracted supernaturals, so it made sense for the council to meet here.

They met in similar buildings placed on the rivers of magic around the world.

It was three stories of nondescript gray cinder blocks with few windows. Zeus navigated the rental van to an underground parking garage.

Drym helped me from the back and the rest of the 'fangs fell out with deadly precision. It struck me again the way they moved, the way they held themselves, the way their awareness swept every inch of their surroundings. It marked them as what they were. Monsters who specialized in killing.

And yet, surrounded by them, I felt safer than I ever had.

Zeus led the way into the council chambers. The large space spanned the entire top floor. A chunky round table stood in the center, its textured surface reflecting the overhead lights.

The lone person in the room—a woman in a pantsuit—recovered from her initial shock and came forward, holding out her hand to me. I shook it as she introduced herself.

"Hello, I'm Corantine Bellanger. I'm the human representative."

I returned her smile. "Hi Corantine. I'm Kendal McPherson, and these are the wyrfangs." I pointed to each one. "Drym, Kragen, Roul, Thurl, Quin, and Cavi."

She went to shake Drym's hand but I stopped her with a hand on her forearm. "Their claws are like diamond and sharp as razors. Best not to shake."

Her eyes went wide and she nodded quickly.

"Right. I'm sorry, and please, call me Cora."

Kragen's deep voice rumbled behind me. "Where are the others?"

"I'll summon portals for them as they're ready. We thought not to overwhelm the wyrfangs," she chuckled, "but I see now we should have been worried for ourselves. Y'all are impressive."

I smiled up at Drym. "They are, aren't they?"

Her head tilted and the smile dropped from her face. "I'll bring them through now. Would you like to sit?"

She waved a hand at the chairs around the table. Unlike the ones at Superhuman Security, these were one piece, with no space between the back and the seat.

I shook my head. "I'll sit, but these chairs won't accommodate their tails."

Her eyes swung to the offending seating and she frowned. "I'm sorry. We should have thought of that."

Kragen spoke again. "We prefer to stand."

Cora nodded, but she still looked upset about the oversight. I liked her. Her deep southern accent was familiar, and she was quick to smile. The fact that it seemed she was genuinely upset that the 'fangs couldn't sit sealed it for me. Anyone who cared about their comfort like that was okay in my book.

She spoke in a language I didn't know while holding her palms toward the long side wall of the room. Six bright blue circles appeared, evenly spaced down the length. They grew wider and taller until they were ovals spanning from the ceiling to the floor. Embers of white sparked from the swirling edges.

I'd never seen anything like it.

One by one, individuals stepped through the portals. Each of them scanned the room, and they all stopped in their tracks when they saw Drym and his brothers. As they recovered from their initial surprise, they moved toward the table.

The portals winked out behind them, and Cora turned her glowing hands toward the table. It stretched and opened like a clam, going from round to a half circle, the chairs lined up on the other side.

The council members took their seats and faced us. I knew the 'fangs spread out behind me. I could feel their tension. My chair, which was neatly tucked under the round table, now stood in the center of the room.

I felt a little exposed. The way they were all staring at us made me feel like we were facing an inquisition.

Cora broke the silence. "Fellow council members, let me introduce the wyrfangs.

She started at one end of the line and moved to the other.

"Kragen, Roul, Thurl, Drym, Quin, and Cavi."

I was impressed she remembered their names and who was who since they'd shifted so Drym could stand behind me when I took my seat.

Cora turned and faced the council. "Society is represented on this council by Ikram, the dragon representative..."

The large man at the center of the table inclined his head.

I mumbled, "Damn it."

I heard Drym chuckle behind me and knew that he'd guessed that I was pouting because I was being denied seeing a dragon. Again.

She pointed to our far left. "By Tyree Greene, the shifter representative…"

The gorgeous dark-skinned man nodded before Cora shifted her hand to the woman next to him.

"By Khuc, the undead representative," Cora's hand shifted down the line as she introduced the others. "By Cesetrios, the cryptid representative, by Osharus, the mer representative, and by Nindrol Zinvaris, representative of the fae."

My eyes narrowed on the thin man at the end of the table. His slicked-back, jet black hair exposed the tips of his pointed ears. The 'fangs erupted into growls behind me, and I saw the fae's lips tip up at the corners.

He wouldn't find it so amusing when they ripped his heart from his chest.

While we were staring at the fae who'd authorized Willis' experiments, Ikram spoke.

Broad chested and smartly dressed in a dark suit, you could imagine he was the CEO of a powerful company. Until his voice rolled over me like sharp gravel. I changed my mind. He was more mafia don than upper management.

"Who is the woman?"

Drym's heavy hand landed on my shoulder.

"My mate."

His tone made it clear that was the end of the discussion.

FORTY-SIX

MY MUSCLES COILED, READY to leap over Kendal and defend her if they made a move against her, but the dragon simply dipped his chin and moved his gaze to Kragen.

"We have no records of creatures such as yours. Please tell us how you came to be."

Zeus already told the full council how we were made, but I would also want to hear it straight from us.

Kragen nodded and shifted from his position at the end of the line to next to me. Roul and Thurl moved to give him room.

"A man named Robert Willis directed a laboratory whose scientists created us from werewolf and dragon DNA."

"For what purpose?"

That question came from the mer representative.

"Death."

Roul's voice rolled over the room, but the silence didn't last. The council members murmured at each other. The only one not surprised was the fae. He didn't lean into his fellow representatives. He stared at us, a cocky smile still on his lips.

Without Kendal to protect, I would have killed him already.

Kragen elaborated on Roul's answer. "The humans saw us as an elite fighting force. They were going to use us to carry out missions they deemed impossible for human soldiers."

I watched in my peripheral vision as his eyes swung to the far right end of the table.

"The council had a different purpose in mind."

All eyes snapped to us. Ikram stood. "What are you saying? We had no knowledge of this laboratory. We do not condone genetic engineering."

"Most of you, perhaps, but at least one of you knew what was happening. Not only knew that we were being created and trained, held captive and tortured, but authorized and encouraged it."

The dragon's eyes narrowed. "You have proof of this?"

"Yes."

"Who do you accuse of such a crime?" Ikram leaned over the table, his palms braced against the wood, his anger apparent.

"Nindrol Zinvaris."

As a one, the council members' heads swung toward the fae. The smirk never left his face.

"Is this true?"

I could see Ikram's muscles bunching under his suit coat. Red scales rolled from beneath the skin of his neck before disappearing.

The fae turned to face the dragon. "Yes. I knew what Willis was doing."

The merman shoved away from the table, distancing himself from Nindrol with a look of disgust on his features.

"It is against Society!"

The dragon's roar made me wince. Kragen's clear voice entered the space that followed.

"We were designed, not to go against all of Society, but one species in particular."

The smile dropped from the fae's face and he went a shade paler as our eyes caught Ikram's.

The dragon slowly turned his head to face Nindrol, the scales beneath his skin crashing like waves against rock. The fae's chair slid across the floor as he stood.

"The humans sought a supernatural solution to their trickier military problems. I authorized their experiments for that alone!"

The flash of red along Ikram's neck continued. He never took his eyes from Nindrol as he asked us, "Do you have proof of these accusations as well?"

Kragen stepped forward. "We are the proof."

The dragon shook his head, but Kragen's next words stopped him.

"Our fur is thick and protects us from heat. We are fast and nimble, able to outmaneuver larger opponents. We have the healing capabilities of shifters. But the one thing we have which was designed specifically for us to use against dragons—are our claws."

Kragen nodded at Roul, who strode to the table. I only then noticed that the surface was covered in dragon scales. He dragged his hand down the length of the table with little effort, leaving behind deep gashes.

I heard a snap and the other five council members jumped from their seats and ran to our end of the room. The table slid across the floor as the dragon shifted, his bulk shredding his clothes and his tail lashing furiously against the back wall.

It felt like the entire building shook with his wrath. He advanced on the fae, who backed until he was pressed against the wall.

"I had no idea they were capable of doing that!"

The dragon's maw opened, and the scales on his throat glowed. "Nindrol Zinvaris, you are relieved of your council seat."

I scooped Kendal into my arms and backed to the far corner of the room. A stream of fire erupted from the dragon. It was smaller, more targeted and controlled than that of the dragon from the day before.

The fae screamed as it hit him, reducing him to a pile of ash in moments.

As Ikram shrunk to his human form, the merman extinguished the last of the flames with his bare feet.

The witch snapped her fingers and conjured a pair of loose sweatpants for the dragon, who stood with his chest heaving and his hands clenched in tight fists. He stepped around the table and his gaze swept the six of us.

I shoved Kendal behind me as he stalked toward us. He stopped short at the movement, his face falling.

"I cannot say I regret the actions of the fae, because that would say I regret your existence. I am sorry you entered this world the way you did. No creature deserves to be caged and used for another's whim.

"I am deeply sorry for that. From this point forward, the wyrfang is a recognized Society species, afforded the full rights and privileges equal to any other. You will be represented by the shifter on the council."

He took a deep breath and shook out his hands.

"Dragons owe you a debt of gratitude for uncovering Nindrol's plot, and as such, we are honored to shelter and provide anything you may need to thrive and enjoy your freedom."

"We appreciate your recognition. Zeus and his team have assisted in providing us all we need. The only thing we might further seek is a purpose."

Kragen glanced over his shoulder at us, and we nodded in agreement.

Ikram copied the move, looking to where his fellow council members were standing before returning his attention to us.

"The council would be grateful if you loaned us your unique skill set occasionally. Zeus has also expressed interest in having your help on troublesome cases."

"Of course."

The dragon nodded. "Cora, a portal to the Seelie fae, please."

The blue oval sprang to life and Ikram walked through without a backward glance.

The other council members left shortly after saying their goodbyes. Cora hesitated before handing Kendal a card.

"Call me if you need anything," she said. "Or even if you want to grab a coffee."

The two women smiled at each other before the witch disappeared through her own portal.

"Well," Kendal said into the silence, "that was exciting. And exhausting. Let's go home."

Quin laughed as we made our way to the parking garage.

"You shouldn't complain, Kendal. You got to see a dragon after all."

FORTY-SEVEN

I FLOPPED BACK INTO the sheets, aftershocks from my latest orgasm still twitching through my body as I fought to catch my breath. Drym laid next to me, his silicone covered claws running up and down my belly.

The council expedited the construction of our houses, and now all six stood scattered on the preserve. The other 'fangs were close enough to visit, but far enough to afford each some long overdue privacy.

We still gathered for meals in the common hall, though it had become more of a war room than a dining room. Corkboards covered one wall, each papered in printouts and maps sporting pins marking possible lab locations.

A movable dry erase board was covered in conspiracy theory style scribbles.

We knew BioSynth lived on. We just didn't know what name they now used or where they'd scurried off to. We'd had no further communications from Isabelle.

Roul had withdrawn further as the weeks passed.

I often wished there was a way for us to reach out to her. I was sure if she knew how badly he was hurting, she would come back.

But those were problems for tomorrow. Tonight was for us.

Drym's low voice rumbled in my ear. "Have I told you lately how beautiful you are?"

"Not for at least thirty minutes."

"Then I have been remiss." He trailed a dulled claw down the side of my face. Goosebumps sprouted on my arms.

He tapped the covered claws against my chest.

"I appreciate your gift."

"I think I appreciate it more." With the coverings, he could explore my body with his hands without fear of cutting me to ribbons. I had to guide him sometimes, but he was a very attentive student.

My gift had definitely benefited me far more than it had him.

"I wanted to return the gesture."

I rolled onto my side and propped my head on my hand. "You got me a gift?"

His ears flicked, and I knew he was nervous. I tried to look behind him, but I would have had to crawl over him to see anything.

"Yes, but they won't be here until tomorrow."

"They?"

He nodded. "The other mates are going to visit."

I squealed so loud his hands flew up to cover his ears. I tossed myself into his arms and covered his chest with kisses as he fell onto his back.

"You like your gift?"

"I love it! How did you convince the shifters to let them come?"

Drym winced. "They are coming with them. We will wait outside so you can visit privately, but none of us will go far."

I slid down his body, notching his still hard cock at my entrance. "That's okay. I like you staying close to me."

I sank onto him and we both groaned. Our bond lights danced and pulsed around us, reflecting the depth of love I held for this beast.

The monster who spent the rest of the night showing me just how much he loved me back.

The next morning, giddy with excitement, I nearly ran to the common hall. Drym's hand in mine was all that held me back.

I barreled through Behemoth and another shifter I had only met once before who stood outside the door. Drym let me go and as the door closed behind me, an intense shyness took over.

The two brunettes in front of me smiled and I waved.

"Hi!" I was breathless from my near run.

The slightly shorter one rushed forward and threw her arms around me.

"Hi back! I'm Virginia, that's Gaelynn, and we are so happy to finally meet you!"

She released me and I saw Gaelynn shaking her head. "Don't mind her. She's thrilled we have another member of the S.M.C."

"S.M.C.?"

Virginia laughed. "The Society Mates Club! We needed three to really call it a club. There aren't many of us, you know. We're a kind of recent phenomenon."

"Oh, that's right. I remember something about shifters' fated mates being not a thing for a while?"

Gaelynn nodded. "Yeah, Fenrir pissed off the fates, but I guess he's been forgiven. Either that, or they got sick of the work required to keep shifters from finding their mates."

"My bet's on the latter. I can't imagine any pissed off woman forgiving that behavior."

We both nodded at Virginia's assessment.

She gasped and spun around. After digging in a gigantic bag for a minute, she emerged with a bundle of fabric. She shook out a t-shirt and grinned before handing it to me. It was a plain white tee with block letters on the back like a football jersey. It read "S.M.C." and beneath that was my first name, followed by WF.

Tears sprang to my eyes as they turned around to show me the backs of their shirts. Virginia's name was followed by WS and Gaelynn's by BS. I knew right away they stood for wyrfang, wolf shifter and bear shifter.

When they turned back around, they were both grinning at me.

"Welcome to the first meeting of the Society Mates Club."

EPILOGUE

"IS IT DONE? IS it really over?"

Drym nodded, a huge grin splitting his lips.

It took five months, but we managed to track down all of the other members of Mr. Blue's hunting club.

It actually only took a few hours for Bull to ferret out their real identities. Once we knew Mr. Blue's real name, those associated with him were easier to find. The other two main assholes—Mr. Red and Mr. Yellow—were the easiest, but Bull's skill was impressive and he found them all, right down to Mr. E and Mr. F.

What took longer was running them to ground. Turns out, rich assholes have a lot of resources to call up when they know they're being hunted.

The wyrfangs finally got their international mission. A couple of the targets escaped to other countries, but with Zeus's help (and his private jet) the 'fangs made swift work of them.

Mr. C evaded the longest. He was smarter than the others and went completely off grid. Cashed out his bank accounts and disappeared into South America.

I still didn't know how Bull located him. When I asked he mumbled something about owing Bacon three pounds of mealworms.

Drym and his brothers were gone for a week. They couldn't move fast through thick jungle and remain hidden.

But now, they were back, crowded around me in the common hall. And I never had to worry the men who hunted me would do it to another woman ever again.

I launched myself into his arms and he caught me.

Quin shouted, "Group hug!" and the others moved close, wrapping their arms around us as well.

I laughed and squeezed Drym harder. My heart burst with happiness. Not only at the rich assholes all being dead, but because the once touch avoidant 'fangs were now cuddlier than a pile of puppies.

Sure, they were cuddly maneaters, but they were *my* cuddly maneaters.

"Take me home." I'd whispered in Drym's ear, but I knew the others heard.

We were released and Drym sprinted to our house on the far side of the compound. He didn't stop until he reached our bedroom, tossing me on the bed.

I laughed. "Did you miss me?"

Drym growled. "Every second."

"Want to show me how much?"

He chuckled. "More than anything."

He showed me how much he missed me in new and inventive ways until I was too wrung out to move.

His cold nose trailed up my neck. "I am yours. You hold my heart, body, and soul in your hands to do with what you wish. I am yours to command. Yours to touch. Yours to—"

I put my finger over his lips. "Love. Mine to love. And I am yours."

Our bond lights glowed so brightly around us that we both closed our eyes.

We still worked to uncover everyone associated with BioSynth. Even Bull was having trouble tracking them.

They couldn't hide forever, and when they surfaced, we'd be ready.

Until then, I would focus on the gentle, loving monster in my bed.

GIVE MOUSE A TREAT

Mouse would be very pleased if you'd leave a review and let us know what you thought. It doesn't have to be long or elaborate, just a few words or a sentence would mean the world to us. (He gets a special treat every time I get a review.)

(That's not the only time he gets treats.
I'm not a monster.)

THANK YOU

Thank you for reading Held by a Monster! I sincerely hope you enjoyed Drym and Kendal's story.

Subscribe to my newsletter for updates and snippets, plus other bonus goodies:https://kenziekelly.com/subscribe

If you just want to know when I have a new release, follow me on Amazon and they'll email you when a new book is available.

This book was professionally edited and proofread, but typos are like rabbits, they multiply when you aren't looking. If you find one, please copy it and the sentence so I can find it and email me at herself@kenziekelly.com.

ABOUT THE AUTHOR

Kenzie grew up in Bluff Park, a suburb of Birmingham, AL in a very improper Southern household. She now lives in a suburb Northeast of Atlanta, GA. She married her college sweetheart and has two sons. She is adored by a Pit Bull and tolerated by two cats. She drinks far too much Diet Coke and feels like she can tackle anything as long as she has a book showing her how.

Though other interests have come and gone, four obsessions have remained constant: horses, photography, reading, and writing.

Her job as chief child wrangler and household CEO consumed most of her energy (creative and otherwise) until April 2017 when the characters in her head demanded their stories be told. She's been writing ever since.

Also by Kenzie:
   The Ka'atari Warriors Series (Sci-Fi Romance)
   The Superhuman Security Series (Paranormal Romance)
   The Whiskey Vex Series (Urban Fantasy)
   The Empyrean Series (Romantic Fantasy)

   For a full, up-to-date list of books, visit her website:
   https://kenziekelly.com.

All rights reserved. No part of this publication may be reproduced, stored in a retrieval system, or transmitted in any form or by any means, electronic, mechanical, recording or otherwise, without the prior written permission of the copyright holder.

Made in United States
Cleveland, OH
10 September 2025